MURDER IN BLACK TIE

MURDER IN BLACK TIE

SARA ROSETT

McGuffin Ink

MURDER IN BLACK TIE

Book Four in the High Society Lady Detective series

Published by McGuffin Ink

ISBN: 978-1-950054-16-9

Copyright © 2019 by Sara Rosett

Cover Design: Alchemy Book Covers

Editing: Historical Editorial

Cast of Characters Illustration by L. Rosett

 Created with Vellum

ACKNOWLEDGMENTS

To my faithful Patreon supporters,

Kelly Biggs
Carol S. Bisig
Margaret Hulse
Connie Hartquist Jacobs
Carolyn Schrader

Thank you so much for supporting me—that's such a simple sentence but every word of it is heart-felt. You're the best!

And thanks to Jami and Danielle. Few things bring me as much joy in my writer life as talking books over chips and guacamole with you two!

CAST OF CHARACTERS

Family Members

Olive Belgrave - discreet problem solver for the high society set

Gwen Stone - Olive's sweet-tempered cousin who runs the domestic side of Parkview Hall

Sir Leo Stone - baronet and owner of Parkview Hall; likes hunting and maps

Lady Caroline Stone - Sir Leo's wife; interested in painting and nudging Gwen into matrimony

Peter Stone - Olive's cousin; survived the war without physical injuries but has episodes

Cecil Belgrave - Olive's father (and Lady Caroline's brother); always lost in his books, either reading them or thinking about his own book

Sonia Belgrave - Olive's managing stepmother

Houseguests

Dinah Lacey (Deena) - heiress; likes couture, jewels, and motors; owns a parrot named Mr. Quigley

Inspector Lucas Longly - Scotland Yard inspector; reserved gentleman with an impeccable family background; he and Gwen have been exchanging letters while she was in the South of France

Captain Thomas Inglebrook - dashing gentleman Gwen met in the South of France

Miss Marion Miller - dithery spinster; often joins Lady Caroline for bridge

Lady Gina Alton (Gigi) - a chum from Olive and Gwen's finishing school days; sultry and interested in fashion and fun

Vincent Payne - gentleman; thinks everyone should acquire one of the antique maps he sells

Jasper Rimington - a family friend; gentleman about town with an unflappable demeanor who often helps Olive in her discreet inquiries

Staff

Brimble - butler

Hannah - maid assigned to Olive

Ross - gardener who also doubles as estate's chauffeur

Grigsby - Jasper's gentleman's gentleman

Mr. Davis - Sir Leo's steward

CHAPTER ONE

NOVEMBER, 1923

*T*he slash of red stood out against the brown and beige of the November countryside. I tightened my gloved hands on the steering wheel and squinted through the window screen of the Morris Cowley to get a better view, but I lost sight of the bright splash of color as the road dipped.

I navigated around the sharp bend near the bridge outside the village of Nether Woodsmoor. The river reflected the graceful stone arches along with the gloomy gray clouds. Normally, I would have slowed down at the river, maybe even stopped for a few moments to admire the view, but today I drove on toward the red gash among the trees.

It wasn't too far ahead, almost near the gates to Parkview Hall, which was my destination. My aunt, Lady Caroline, and my cousins, Gwen and Violet, had

1

recently returned from an extended holiday in the South of France. To celebrate their homecoming, Aunt Caroline had extended invitations to a select group of family and friends to stay for a few days.

I slowed. It was a motor, a sleek Alfa Romeo the color of holly berries, its nose in the ditch and tires spinning deeper into the mud. I brought the Morris to a stop and hooked my arm over the door as I leaned out to call, "Everything all right?" My breath made little white puffs.

I could tell from their brightly colored hats that the driver and passenger were women, but they were both turned away from me, and the noise of the engine drowned out my voice.

I gave the horn a sharp blast. The tires stopped turning, and the women twisted to look over their shoulders. "Olive!" My cousin Gwen climbed out and picked her way across the mud. She leaned into my motor and gave me a quick hug. "What perfect timing. You came along at exactly the right moment. Didn't she, Deena?" Gwen turned toward the young woman who had remained in the driver's seat of the Alfa Romeo. "Olive can give us a lift to Parkview, and we'll send Ross to retrieve your motor," Gwen called.

In one of her letters about the upcoming party, Gwen had listed the guests, but I didn't remember Deena's name being on the list.

"Is that Deena Lacey?" I asked Gwen in an undertone. "From Charles Manor?"

Gwen nodded an affirmative.

"I haven't seen her since—oh, I don't know. It must

have been sometime early on during the war." Charles Manor was thirty miles to the north of Parkview Hall. Deena had lived there with her uncle, who was her guardian after her parents died, until she came into her inheritance. When we were children, our paths had crossed occasionally, but since she was four years older —a great gulf when one is a child—we didn't have much in common. "I thought she lived mostly in London."

"She does. She's only recently returned from town," Gwen replied in an equally low voice. "It's a long story."

Deena glanced at the dark gray clouds. "But it looks as if it's about to rain—or snow—and that will only make it worse. I know I can get back on the road. The salesman assured me this motor has excellent handling." Deena revved the engine.

Gwen said to me, "I don't know about that, but I'm sure it was the most expensive one."

"Trying day?" I asked. My cousin Gwen had the sweetest and most long-suffering temperament. If she was out of sorts, then the situation had to be rather dire.

"Deena and I went into the village to shop." Gwen gave her glove a sharp tug. She seemed about to say more but stopped herself.

"So Deena's here at Parkview for the party?"

My last words were drowned out as Deena revved the engine of the Alfa Romeo. Wheels spun, flinging mud that splattered onto the road near the back of the Morris. Gwen took a few quick steps, moving nearer the

Morris's bonnet. I let the Morris roll forward a few feet, out of the range of the mud.

Gwen looked as though she'd like to call Nanny and have her take charge of Deena, but she drew a breath and shouted between the roars of the engine, "Deena, it's only getting worse. Come away. I promise we'll have your motor back at Parkview before dinner."

Deena cut the engine. "Oh, all right. I suppose we'd better. I do hope they're quick about it, though."

"I'll see to it," Gwen said as Deena climbed out of the low motor and slammed the door.

Deena was dressed head to toe in gold. Her hat was the same shade as a sovereign and covered every strand of hair, which highlighted the fact that her face was a long narrow oval. She'd always reminded me of the illustrations in Father's books of Byzantine saints with their elongated faces and mournful expressions. I recognized Deena's hat as one of Madame LaFoy's priciest creations. I'd briefly considered working in the haberdashery, and I'd seen the beautiful cloche with its trailing feathers and embroidery in that establishment. Deena's mink-collared wool driving coat was of the same shade of gold.

She took a few steps on her tiptoes in an effort to keep her gold T-strap shoes out of the mud, but then she stopped and swiveled back to the motor. "Mr. Quigley! We mustn't forget him."

"Mr. Quigley?" I asked Gwen. "Who's Mr. Quigley?" I didn't remember a guest named Mr. Quigley either.

Gwen let out a tiny sigh. "A parrot."

I wasn't sure I'd heard her correctly, but Deena leaned over the side of the motor and lifted out a birdcage. It rocked to the accompaniment of squawks and flapping wings as she minced across the mud. "Don't worry, boy. I've got you." Deena climbed up the bank of sodden grass. A moment before she reached us, her foot slipped, and she pitched forward. Gwen caught her elbow and an edge of the birdcage.

Deena said, "Whoops! Thank you, Gwen."

Inside the cage, the bird rotated its head and fixed an eye on Gwen's fingers. She jerked her hand back.

"Oh, you don't have to worry about Mr. Quigley. He never bites." Deena propped the cage on the edge of the door at my eye level. "Hello, Olive. Isn't he just the most gorgeous thing you've ever seen?"

Mr. Quigley rocked on his perch. "He's not brightly colored," I said.

The feathers fluffed up around his head and neck, as if he were displaying the gradual transition of color from nearly white at his head to a pearly gray at the tips of his wings. His tail feathers were a bright red. "No, he's an African Gray—an extremely expensive parrot. And the most intelligent too."

Clearly, Deena rated the intelligence of the parrot as of secondary importance compared to the cost. "How did you come to have a parrot?" I asked her.

"I wanted a pet to keep me company, but simply *everyone* has a dog or a cat. I had to have something unusual, something memorable."

"Mr. Quigley certainly is that," I said. Even with his muted coloring, which resembled the clouds today, he looked exotic and out of place in the English country-side. "How long have you had him?"

"Six days. I simply couldn't leave him at Charles Manor. Parrots need plenty of interaction."

Gwen said, "Deena thought Mr. Quigley should see the village."

Mr. Quigley let out a high-pitched whistle that pierced the air.

"Goodness," I said. "What does that mean?"

Deena smiled like an indulgent parent. "He's saying hello."

Gwen said, "He's been doing that for the last hour."

"I see." That sharp noise within a short distance of one's ear would become irritating. "Does he say anything?"

"Oh yes. He's quite chatty. His previous owner spoke to him all the time and trained him to say many things."

"Is it salty language?" I glanced at Gwen. Aunt Caroline wouldn't be happy to have a parrot spouting naughty words during her party.

"Oh no. His former owner was a missionary." Deena addressed the cage. "Say something for us, Mr. Quigley."

Mr. Quigley rocked on his perch, then tucked his beak under his wing.

A wrinkle appeared between Deena's thin brows. "Actually, he hasn't said anything yet. I do hope the man wasn't lying to me about Mr. Quigley being able to speak."

"I doubt it, especially if he was a missionary," Gwen said.

"Well, perhaps Mr. Quigley will talk to us later," I said. "Let's see if we can all get in the Morris. It'll be a crush—"

Deena looked back at her motor. "I do hate to go off and leave the Alfa Romeo. It's lonely out here. Do you think it will be all right?"

"Of course. No one will bother it," Gwen said.

Deena gripped her mink collar with one hand and drew it closer around her neck. "Perhaps I should stay while you two go and get help."

"Don't be a goose," Gwen said, her voice firm. "It will be perfectly fine. Now let's get out of this cold."

"I suppose we should—" Deena looked beyond Gwen's shoulder and asked, "Look, isn't that Inspector Longly and Captain Inglebrook? There, moving through the shadows of the trees. The shoot must be over." Deena waved. "Yoo-hoo!"

I knew Detective Inspector Longly from Scotland Yard. I recognized his silhouette with his empty sleeve pinned against his jacket. The other man was taller with broader shoulders. As they came out from under the trees, I could see he had a pencil mustache and dark hair.

"I'm anxious to meet Captain Inglebrook," I said, giving Gwen a significant glance.

She'd written to me several weeks ago in a state, which wasn't like her at all. She had a calm methodical nature and wasn't given to flights of fancy or emotional upheaval, but the idea of the two male houseguests,

Inspector Longly and Captain Inglebrook, had her flustered.

She'd met Captain Inglebrook in France. The holiday was an effort to help Violet recover her equilibrium after a rather horrifying incident at Archly Manor, which was where we'd met Inspector Longly. I'd thought there was an attraction between Gwen and Inspector Longly, but then Gwen's letters from France had frequently mentioned Captain Inglebrook while Longly's name had been largely absent. Upon their return to Parkview, Violet, fully recovered from her trauma and back to her usual mischievous ways, had engineered invitations for both men, causing Gwen endless amounts of distress. At this moment, Gwen didn't look eager to speak to either man. I couldn't wait to get her alone and see what had happened.

"Captain Inglebrook's gaze is positively smoldering," Deena said. "It makes me feel like I'm going to swoon every time I'm near him." Deena shoved the cage into Gwen's arms and hurried down the road to the men.

"She certainly doesn't look as if she's about to swoon now," I said. "More like she's running a fifty-yard dash."

"She has quite the sturdy constitution," Gwen said. "If only she had as much sense as she has money and energy." Mr. Quigley inched toward Gwen's fingers. She set the cage down and stepped back.

"Didn't Deena say he doesn't bite?"

"I'm not taking any chances," Gwen said. "My only experience with pets is rather mundane, dogs and cats and a few horses. I don't know what to do with an exotic bird."

The men and Deena strolled up to us. She had her arm through Captain Inglebrook's elbow and looked as if she'd won a prize at the village fete. Both Inglebrook and Longly were dressed in tweed and their cheeks were bright red from the cold.

The captain disengaged himself from Deena as Gwen introduced me. Captain Inglebrook had raven black hair smoothed back from a handsome square face. His dark gaze fastened on me as if I were the only woman for miles around as he shook my hand then placed his other hand on top of it. "Good afternoon, Miss Belgrave. It's a delight to meet London's lovely lady detective. I've heard about your illustrious career."

"Captain Inglebrook, I see already that you tend to exaggeration, and I shouldn't believe a word of what you say."

"On the contrary. Everyone is talking about you. You're brilliant."

"Hardly. I'm sure Inspector Longly would disagree," I said lightly to draw the inspector into the conversation. He stood a few steps back from the others. Longly's posture was more suited to a parade ground and didn't go with the casual atmosphere of the group gathered around the Morris. I'd only encountered Longly when he was working, and I'd expected his manner to be less restrained here at Parkview while he was off duty.

"Miss Belgrave does indeed have some interesting

insights." Longly's tone was matter-of-fact and seemed at odds with Inglebrook's teasing banter.

Inglebrook didn't seem to take notice of Longly's flat tone and transferred his attention to the birdcage. "Did Mr. Quigley enjoy his trip?"

"He charmed everyone we met, didn't he, Gwen?" Deena said.

Gwen made a noise that could possibly be construed as agreement.

Deena gripped Captain Inglebrook's arm and pulled him down the slope to the Alfa Romeo. "You must help. My poor motor. I hate to leave it out here in such a lonely place."

Captain Inglebrook surveyed the scene. "What happened?"

"I don't know," Deena said. "We were going along just fine, then suddenly we were in the ditch."

"It's a shame." Inglebrook ran his gloved hand over the red paint. "It's a fine machine. Any damage?" Deena and Inglebrook walked around to examine the bonnet.

Inspector Longly said, "Ladies," put on his hat that he'd removed when he approached, then went over to Deena's motor. He climbed in and motioned for Inglebrook to crank the engine. Once the motor was running, he called out for Deena and Inglebrook to stand aside. Instead of trying to reverse through the gouges in the mud that Deena had made, Longly inched the motor forward until it was on slightly drier ground. He made a sweeping turn, accelerated up the slope, and bumped onto the road.

Deena clapped her hands. "Brilliant, Inspector Longly! I never thought of going forward." Deena took Captain Inglebrook's arm and tugged him up the incline to the road. "Let's all ride back to Parkview together." Longly began to climb out, but Deena waved him back. "No, stay. We can all squeeze in. You *must* drive. I'm too flustered." Deena called to Gwen and me over her shoulder, "Take good care of Mr. Quigley." Once they were settled with Deena seated between the two men, the red motor accelerated away.

Gwen watched them for a moment, then murmured, "Something's wrong."

"Inspector Longly seemed a bit withdrawn," I ventured.

"Yes, he is." A combination of irritation and puzzlement infused Gwen's tone as her gaze tracked the car. "But it's more than that. There's an atmosphere—a tension—" She shook her head, which caused the tendrils of her fair hair that had escaped from her bun to shift about her face. "I don't know."

"What do you mean?" This was more than Gwen being irritated with a trying houseguest, and she wasn't the sort of person who worried needlessly, fretting over minor details and blowing up little incidents into phantom problems.

The Alfa Romeo disappeared through the Parkview gates, and Gwen's brow lowered into a frown. "I can't describe it, except to say the atmosphere is rather fraught." She shrugged. "Perhaps you'll be able to figure it out. You're much better at these intuitive, under-the-surface things." Returning to her normal good-natured manner, she looked down at the birdcage. "It appears Mr. Quigley and I have been abandoned. Can you give us a lift?"

"I think I can squeeze you and Mr. Quigley in," I said as Gwen picked up the birdcage and went around to the passenger side.

"Goodness. What's all this?" Gwen's gaze ranged over the passenger seat of the motor, which was stuffed with my luggage. The dickey seat was packed as well with my trunk and more boxes. "What's happened?" A smile lit up her face. "Are you moving back to Nether Woodsmoor?"

"No, far from it. At least, I hope not—as much as I'd like to be near you, living with Father and Sonia is just too grim to contemplate. Climb in and I'll explain all."

CHAPTER TWO

*W*e shuffled my belongings around to make room, then Gwen settled into the motor with a valise on her lap. As I put the Morris in gear, she looked over Mr. Quigley's cage, which was positioned between us. "So if you're not moving back to Nether Woodsmoor, what's happened? Don't tell me you've been kicked out of the boardinghouse."

"Essentially, yes. Mrs. Gutler is getting married. She's been seeing a very nice bachelor who also owns a house. They decided to put her boardinghouse on the market, and she's moving in with him as soon as they're married. So I no longer have a place to live in London—well, after next week I don't. I hoped I could store some of my belongings at Parkview until I sort out new living arrangements."

"Of course. This is something you want kept quiet, I take it?"

"Heavens, yes. Please don't mention it to Father or Sonia." My father was a retired vicar and had been a widower for over a decade, but then Sonia came along and changed everything.

"They won't hear a word from me. Have you looked for other lodgings?"

"Yes, but no luck there. I do have a bit of money saved, and I thought I could afford a small flat."

"You can't?"

"The absolute best place I've seen is a basement flat only slightly larger than a wardrobe with the wallpaper curling away from the wall because of the damp." I navigated the motor through Parkview's gates, then turned to the right onto the road that branched off the main drive and looped around the wooded grounds of the estate, which would give us time to chat. We rolled along the long tree-lined road, the bare limbs of the oaks and elms creating a stencil against the gray sky.

Mr. Quigley let out a squawk followed by a stream of clicking sounds. I jumped, and the steering wheel vibrated as the motor drifted to the edge of the lane, churning up gold, red, and yellow leaves. I adjusted the wheel, bringing the Morris fully back onto the road. Mr. Quigley trotted back and forth on his perch and spread his wings.

"I think he likes my driving," I said. "Enough about me. I'm sure I'll sort out something." I ignored the throb of worry that had grown stronger as I fruitlessly searched London for a new room. I pushed away those thoughts. "So what's this about the atmosphere at Parkview?"

Gwen shifted on the seat and gripped the valise tighter. "I don't know. Everyone seems so . . . *on edge* is the only way to describe it. There's tension between Inspector Longly and Captain Inglebrook."

I cut my gaze to her. "I can tell you why that is."

She gave a little laugh. "It's not me, if that's what you think."

"Are you sure?"

"Absolutely. From the moment he arrived, Inspector Longly has made it clear he's not interested in me at all." Her voice caught on the last words. She looked away out the window.

"Are you sure?" I asked over Mr. Quigley's clicking sounds. "When I saw Inspector Longly at Blackburn Hall, he was anxious for any details I could share about you. Men generally don't act like that unless they're interested in a lady."

"Perhaps he was interested at one time, but that's certainly not the case now. He's made that *abundantly* clear, despite all his letters."

"Letters?"

"We wrote to each other while I was away."

That was news to me. Gwen hadn't mentioned she was corresponding with Longly. "How often?"

"A few times a week."

"I see."

"And he was so different when we met in London for tea."

"You met in London?" That was interesting as well. Apparently, things between her and Longly had progressed much farther than I'd realized.

"Yes, Mother had several appointments in town, and I went up with her. I'd mentioned I'd be there, and

Inspector Longly suggested tea." Her voice softened. "We met at a little tea shop in Piccadilly and strolled in the park afterwards. A few days later he invited me to dinner. We had a lovely time."

I was pleased for her. "So you have a sweetheart."

"Don't be cross that I didn't tell you. I didn't tell *anyone*."

"Not even Aunt Caroline?"

"Especially not Mother. I would have told you, but —I know it sounds silly—but I thought if I told anyone I'd jinx it. It all felt exactly right. I didn't want to spoil it, but somehow it's all gone wrong."

"Have you and Inspector Longly argued? Had a disagreement?"

She shook her head. "He's hardly spoken to me since he arrived."

"I'm sorry, Gwen."

She lifted one shoulder. Her throat worked up as she swallowed. "It's fine. Really, it is," she said in a choked voice.

Clearly, it was far from fine. It was just like Gwen to keep her growing fondness for the inspector to herself. The fact that she hadn't told me about it meant she did indeed care about him. "He's an imbecile if he doesn't want you."

Mr. Quigley chirped, then announced, "Foolishness of fools is folly."

After a startled second, we both giggled. Gwen said, "So Mr. Quigley does talk. Was that a quote?"

"From Proverbs, I think."

"Deena did say he was owned by a missionary."

"Perhaps Mr. Quigley knows heaps of Bible verses?" I asked in a leading tone as I glanced away from the road to the parrot.

He fixed his small eyes on me but remained silent.

Gwen put her hand to her chest. "Oh my. What if he's a scripture-quoting parrot? I think that's much more exotic than Deena wanted."

We tried to coax another phrase out of Mr. Quigley, but he twisted his head around and gave his attention to grooming the feathers on his wing, so I said, "Tell me about Captain Inglebrook."

"He's as charming as ever," Gwen said, her voice flat.

"Perhaps a little too charming?" I asked, thinking of the captain's lingering gaze when we were introduced and the way he'd held my hand, almost caressing it. "Bit of a Don Juan?"

"More than a bit. A legendary one, I believe." She ran her finger along a seam on the valise. "When we met him in France, he was so amiable and entertaining, but now . . . he seems—oh, this is terrible to say, but— he seems shallow. He's all surface and gloss. No depth."

"I see." Gwen wasn't the sort of woman who wanted a dalliance. "Well, perhaps Inspector Longly will come around. It's possible he's worried about something to do with his work. A case might be bothering him."

"Perhaps," Gwen said, but she sounded unconvinced.

Irritation at Violet flared inside me. Her matchmaking had gone awry. "I'm surprised Violet didn't go to Nether Woodsmoor with you." I'd never known Violet to pass up a shopping expedition, even if it was only to the village.

"She's not here. She's visiting James's family."

"Oh my. So it is serious."

"Yes. I thought she'd forget all about James in France, but she wrote to him almost every day. He replied just as often, and his letters always cheered her. When we arrived back, she and James picked up exactly where they left off. I think we'll be planning a summer wedding." Gwen said this without any jealousy or envy.

"You really are too sweet-tempered sometimes," I said. "You should be at least a little upset with Violet for putting you in this awkward situation. I wish she hadn't fixed it so that both Inspector Longly and Captain Inglebrook received invitations."

"Oh, I'm not pleased about that," Gwen said quickly, but then her expression softened. "But I do want to see Violet happy. That's more important than a little"—she swished her hand back and forth—"tension in the air for a few days."

"You may feel like that, but I want to have a little chat with Violet. She needs to stop interfering." I shook off the exasperation I felt because this conversation wasn't cheering Gwen up. She still had the worried furrow between her brows. "Tell me, who's here? Has everyone arrived?" I asked, hoping to distract her.

Gwen touched her fingers as she ticked off names. "Inspector Longly. Captain Inglebrook. Gigi—although

I haven't seen much of her. She didn't come down until two o'clock today."

"That sounds like the Gigi we know." Gigi—Lady Gina Alton—had been at finishing school with us. Gigi skated along the surface of life, her focus on fashion, makeup, and her own comfort, but she was great fun. Except for our paths crossing for a few moments at parties, I hadn't seen her in ages.

"Miss Miller made her disapproval of Gigi quite clear."

"That name sounds vaguely familiar."

"She's a friend of mother's, a dithery spinster who lived with her brother until he passed away last year. She has a tendency to ramble on. Peter was her partner for bridge last night, and he was marvelously patient. Thank goodness she wasn't partnered with Father. Nothing irritates him more than someone who hesitates and second-guesses, which is how Miss Miller plays every hand."

The road branched again, and I took the left fork, which would wind through the trees and back to Parkview. "How is Peter?"

"Better—*much* better. It's such a relief to Mother and Father. Peter seems—well, almost back to normal. He's taken an interest in the estate, and Father's handed off the management of several areas to him. Peter doesn't seem as nervous as he used to. He's finally sleeping better too, which is a great help."

"I'm pleased to hear it." Peter had served in the Great War and had come home without a single injury —at least, no visible injuries. It was only after he'd been back for a few months that we all began to realize he was suffering from what he'd seen—nightmares and a mental anguish none of us could understand.

Gwen continued, "And of course your father and Sonia will be here tonight for dinner, if she's feeling up to it. They came for tea but had to leave because Sonia wasn't feeling well."

"Not feeling well? Sonia?" That combination of words didn't make sense. I slowed the motor and turned to Gwen to make sure I'd heard her correctly over the noise of the engine. Sonia had the constitution of a Clydesdale horse and the tenacity of a mosquito. I couldn't imagine her ill. She'd overpower any sickness with the force of her will—it simply wouldn't be allowed. She'd been a nurse—Father's nurse, in fact—before they married. I imagined she bullied her patients back to wellness.

"I don't know what was wrong," Gwen said. "Sonia was very pale. They left shortly after everyone arrived for tea."

Sonia was my least favorite person in the world, but I didn't want her to be ill. Even though I couldn't imagine what Father saw in Sonia, he was fond of her. If she were ill, he'd be distressed. I hadn't stopped at Tate House when I drove through the village because I knew Father and Sonia were to be guests at Parkview for a few days, and I'd thought I'd see them there. I'd have to send a note around and check on them once I was settled at Parkview.

"Who have I forgotten?" Gwen tilted her head as

she ran through a mental list. "Oh yes. Mr. Vincent Payne."

"Another unknown for me."

"For me as well. Father is interested in some maps Mr. Payne inherited from his grandfather. You know Father and his maps."

"Yes, like your mother and her painting." Aunt Caroline spent every free moment painting landscapes of the surrounding countryside—at least that's what she told us they were. To me, her oil paintings looked like blobs and splotches—something akin to a blotting paper—but I wasn't artistic. Perhaps her paintings were quite good, and I was just quite dense and couldn't see it. Uncle Leo, on the other hand, didn't create. He had two main interests, hunting and collecting maps. Because of his interest in maps, the library at Parkview had nearly as many maps as it did books, and scholars often visited to study them.

"And is Mr. Payne as old and dusty as his maps?" I asked, thinking he might make a good dinner partner for Miss Miller.

"Hardly. He's . . . well, he's hard to describe."

"What is it?" I asked. "I can tell from your tone that there's something else—something unflattering—and you don't want to mention it, but it's bothering you. You can tell me. I won't pass it on."

"Well—" Gwen swiveled so she faced me. "He's . . . pushy. Father wants to buy his maps. In fact, I *know* Father will buy his maps, but Mr. Payne keeps going on and on about how rare and valuable they are and how

Father *must* have them. And this morning, I didn't want to take a stroll in the garden with him, but he insisted."

"And you were too nice to make an excuse."

"He's a guest."

"A pushy guest. You don't owe him anything—a walk in the garden or anything else."

"I know that, but he looked devastated when I said I had to look over the menus, which wasn't a lie."

"Oh, I know it wasn't a lie." Aunt Caroline could be lost in the clouds, especially when it came to her painting, and she left much of the day-to-day running of Parkview to Gwen. "So he's pushy and manipulative."

"Now I've given you a dislike of him."

"You've done nothing of the sort, only given me a bit of a warning. I'll be perfectly polite to him. Thank goodness I'm not in the market for antique maps."

"And then there's Deena," Gwen said.

"Yes. I didn't know she would be here. You didn't mention her in your letter."

"It was a last moment thing. Mother and I were at Lady Smith-Wentworth's card party a few days ago. I went to the withdrawing room to retie my sash, and Deena was crying in a corner. She was engaged to Mr. Cathcart, you know."

"Cathcart? Eddie Cathcart, who I heard last week is engaged to Miss Felicity Knight?"

"Yes, *that* Eddie Cathcart. The news of his engagement to Miss Knight came out during the card party."

"How awful for Deena," I said. "That explains her sudden return to Charles Manor."

"Yes, she wanted to escape the rumors and the speculation and the pitying looks, I'm sure. Of course, after a slight delay, the news did reach Nether Woodsmoor."

"One would suppose someone of her fortune wouldn't have trouble holding onto a fiancé," I said.

"Miss Knight's fortune is even larger than Deena's."

"I see. Then it's sad that Mr. Cathcart is a cad and a fortune hunter. At least that's something we'll never have to worry about—fortune hunters, I mean. Me, less than you." Except for my small bit of savings, I was penniless. While Gwen would have a nice dowry, the estate of Parkview was entailed and would go to Peter.

"Thank you for pointing out a blessing I didn't realize I had."

"It's good to see you smile," I said in reply to her joking tone. "In all seriousness, though, Deena's had a lucky escape if that was the only reason Mr. Cathcart was marrying her."

"You and I can see that, and I think she's coming around to that view, but that wasn't how she felt at Lady Smith-Wentworth's card party. I do feel sorry for her. She spends so much time trying to be fashionable and—well, to be like Gigi—but she doesn't quite . . ."

"No. She doesn't have Gigi's flair. Deena is trying *too* hard. If she'd relax and be herself, I'm sure it would all be fine."

"Yes, I suppose so," Gwen said as I turned the wheel, bringing the motor around a gradual curve. Woods spread out on each side of the road, dense thickets of trees and drifts of fallen leaves.

Several yards ahead of us, a woman in a full-length fur coat emerged from the trees at the side of the road.

She didn't glance in our direction as she stalked down the road away from us in the direction of Parkview.

"That's Gigi," Gwen said, surprise in her tone. There was no mistaking Gigi's petite frame and gorgeously cut designer coat. "What's she doing way out here?"

Gigi wasn't one for long rambles. The only type of strolling she did was along Bond Street as she went from shop to shop. I eased my foot off the accelerator as I pulled alongside Gigi and called a greeting.

Gigi came over to the Morris. Two midnight black curls peeked out from under her hat brim and lay against her cheeks. "Oh, hello! I was lost in my own little world and didn't hear the motor. It's lovely to see you, Olive."

Gwen leaned over the birdcage. "Gigi, what are you doing?"

"I'm out for a walk. It's what one does in the country, isn't it? One wanders around in the bracing air, admiring the trees and shrubbery and such."

A man hurried out of the trees, his suit jacket flapping as he ran, exposing a bit of a paunch that pressed against his waistcoat. Gigi turned away from him and resumed her quick pace up the road. I let the motor roll forward alongside her. "Do you want a ride? I'm not sure where we'll put you, but—"

"Gigi!" the man called as he jogged up to us. "Please, wait a moment."

Gigi whirled to face the man, who looked to be in his early thirties and had light brown hair and brown eyes that matched the tweed he wore. "Yes, Mr. Payne?"

I stepped on the brake. From her sharp tone, it was

obvious Gigi was displeased with Mr. Payne, and I wasn't about to speed away and leave her alone with him.

"Gigi—please—" Winded from his run, Mr. Payne drew in a deep breath, his face perplexed. "I didn't realize—"

Gigi turned to Gwen and me. "Mr. Payne suggested a walk through the grounds."

"Yes, because there was a break in the drizzle" —he gulped air— "and I thought we should take advantage."

"Yes, *you* certainly did." Her words were soft, but I caught them. Gigi had the look of a teacher who'd just cracked a ruler against the knuckles of a naughty student.

Payne looked away from her steady gaze, turning the other side of his face to me for a moment. His left cheek was bright pink. As he swiveled back to Gigi, his expression transitioned, a contrite look replacing puzzlement. "If I've offended, I apologize."

Gigi gave a sharp nod as a breeze stirred, rippling her mink coat. The bare tree limbs overhead rattled, and leaves skittered across the ground.

Gwen cleared her throat. "Olive, I don't believe you've met our guest. This is Mr. Vincent Payne. He's brought some rather spectacular antique maps with him from London to show Father. Mr. Payne, this is my cousin, also up from London, Miss Olive Belgrave."

Payne's face immediately transformed again into a wide smile, which deepened the dimple in his chin as he removed his trilby. "How do you do?"

It seemed Payne had one of those mobile faces that could shift through expressions, instantly altering his features. "Very well, Mr. Payne," I said. "I'm glad to be here at Parkview after a long drive from London."

"That's right!" He pointed at me. "You're the brainy detective lady."

I felt as if I were an animal at a zoo as he gawked at me.

"We're safe as houses now with you here," he said as he stared. "I've never seen a lady detective. Well, now I don't have to worry about anyone pinching my maps—they're extremely rare, you know. If any criminals are around, just the word of your arrival will send them packing."

"I'm sure there are no criminals around Parkview," Gwen said.

Payne's grin widened as he scanned the road in an exaggerated manner, his gaze traveling from one end of the lane to the other. "You never know, Miss Stone. That's one thing I've learned—you can never be too careful." He returned his hat to his head and extended his arm to Gigi. "Shall we continue?"

"I don't think so." Gigi stepped onto the running board of the Morris and hooked her elbow along the door. "You don't mind if I catch a ride with you back to Parkview, do you, Olive? These shoes aren't made for tromping around the countryside. I can't walk another step."

"Of course not." I glanced at Payne. "I'm afraid we don't have room inside, but you're welcome to the other running board."

Payne opened his mouth, but Gigi said, "Mr. Payne prefers walking. He assured me earlier of his deep love of country walks."

Payne said, "Er—I do enjoy the out-of-doors on occasion."

"Excellent," Gigi said. "Then we'll see you at the house." She tapped my arm. "Let's go."

I let the motor roll forward, and we left Payne trudging along behind us.

"That was rather mean," Gwen said to Gigi.

Gigi put up her free hand to hold onto her hat as the Morris picked up a bit of speed. "No more than he deserves. I like a little petting as much as the next girl, but he was overfamiliar."

Gwen looked scandalized. "I knew he wasn't a gentleman."

"Don't worry, I can handle men like him." Gigi's eyes flashed. "He won't bother me again."

"It's not you I'm worried about," Gwen said. "I know you can take care of yourself. It's the maids." She leaned back against the seat. "I'll have a word with the staff and make sure none of the maids are left alone with Mr. Payne."

As we neared Parkview, the figures of Longly, Deena, and Inglebrook came into view. The red Alfa Romeo was parked at the foot of the divided staircase that curved to the double doors of the grand house. Deena was still between the two men, her arms linked through theirs as they climbed one branch of the staircase. Even from a distance, I could see the wide smile on her narrow face. "It appears a few days in the country was just what Deena needed," I said to Gwen.

"She does seem to be in better spirits, which is good. But Mother's still upset because the numbers aren't even. We have one too many ladies."

Gigi said, "Your mother is so sweet and old-fashioned. Tell her it's fine. We're used to the shortage of men."

"Mother won't be deterred. She's so relaxed about some things, but she's adamant about having even numbers. Mother would have invited the curate, but he's away."

"Thank goodness for that," I said. "Otherwise, I'm sure Sonia—ill or not—would maneuver me in his direction at every possible opportunity." After Sonia married Father, she'd decided I should also experience wedded bliss and had fixed on the curate as the best local candidate. "What about Mr. Davis?" The bald and rotund estate manager was a pleasant dinner companion.

Mr. Quigley's cage rocked as I swept around the circle drive. Gwen gripped the ring at the top to brace it, keeping her fingers clear of the cage itself. "Mr. Davis is attending to some business for Father in London. Mother sent a note off to Jasper to see if he'll join us to even things up."

"Jasper will be here?" Jasper was Peter's school chum. Because Jasper's father was in civil service and lived abroad, Jasper had spent most of his school holidays at Parkview. A few months ago when our paths crossed in London, Jasper and I had renewed our acquaintance. We met for tea at the Savoy occasionally. A little burst of happiness filled me at the thought of seeing Jasper so soon. "I thought he was off on a shooting trip to Scotland."

"It was cut short for some reason, and he's back. But he won't arrive until tomorrow," Gwen said. "We'll just have an uneven table tonight with thirteen. It's unlucky, but what can we do?"

CHAPTER THREE

*G*igi had no qualms about carrying Mr. Quigley's cage inside, and I dropped her and Gwen at the bottom of one branch of the divided staircase. I drove around to the old stables. By the time my luggage and boxes were unloaded, I'd missed tea, so I headed straight up to my room to change for dinner.

I was in my favorite room. It overlooked the interior courtyard and was decorated with hand-painted Chinese wallpaper and a matching three-panel wooden lacquered screen with the same pattern of bamboo, flowers, and birds. The design of green leaves and flowers in the rug that covered the center of the room echoed the Oriental theme. It had always been "my" room whenever I stayed over at Parkview. Bowls of yellow and white chrysanthemums gave the room a cheerful touch. I imagined Ross, the aged gardener, had cut them this morning, and Gwen had probably arranged them.

It didn't take the maid, a chatty young woman named Hannah, long to unpack my trunk, draw a bath for me, and help me out of my travel clothes. I dismissed her and went through the connecting door to have a long soak. One of the lovely things about the Oriental room was the adjoining bath, a luxury that most rooms didn't have. When the previous Lady Stone had renovated the upstairs, she'd had a linen closet transformed into a bath and created a connecting door between the bath and the Oriental room. Aunt Caroline's predecessor had been determined to modernize the house and created as much useable space as possible during the renovations, which meant that besides overseeing the installation of new baths in each wing, she'd packed as many cubbyholes, nooks, and storage closets into the two wings as possible.

She'd also seen that a door was added to the bath, which opened onto the hallway so other guests could access it. Hannah told me that everyone in this wing had already bathed, so I took my time, luxuriating in the deep tub and trying to work out what could make Longly, who had seemed smitten with Gwen, become so standoffish.

He wasn't fickle. I couldn't believe he'd drop her so quickly. Perhaps Violet had thought Longly would be jealous when he saw Gwen and Inglebrook. If that had been her plan, it had backfired. And even on my short acquaintance with Captain Inglebrook, I could tell he wasn't husband material. I picked up a bar of soap and a sponge. Gwen and Longly hadn't argued, so what could have caused his change in attitude? Had he found out something about Gwen that he found disagreeable? No, I didn't think that was possible. Was it her parents? Uncle Leo and Aunt Caroline each had their eccentricities, but they were lovely people, and I couldn't imagine they hadn't welcomed Longly as a guest. After a bit more ruminating, I gave up and reached for a towel.

I was used to taking care of myself and didn't call for Hannah again when I climbed out of the tub. I chose my teal silk gown with a fitted bodice that flowed over my waist and hips. Intricately embroidered flowers trailed from the bodice down to the swirl of the full skirt. It was one of my oldest gowns—a hand-me-down from Gwen—but it was one of my favorites because of the beautiful detailing.

Dinner this evening was more informal—well, as informal as Aunt Caroline allowed. She'd unbent enough to designate tonight as an evening for the men to wear dinner jackets. For tomorrow's dinner party, tailcoats would be expected, which meant the women would wear their finest couture and jewels. I left my mother's long string of pearls for tomorrow night. Unlike Gigi, who had some spectacular family jewelry, and Deena, who could pick up as many baubles with precious stones as she liked, my accessories were a bit limited. I smoothed my dark bob into place, worked my gloves up over my elbows, and picked up my silk shawl, determined to corner Longly and figure out what had happened to cause such a shift in his manner.

I opened my door and found a plump blonde woman with wide blue eyes, high cheekbones, and white strands threaded through fair hair. She was kneading a handkerchief. "Oh, hello there," I said as I closed the door to my room. "You must be Miss Miller. I'm Miss Belgrave. How do you do?"

"Not good. Not good at all." She glanced first one way, then the other, up and down the corridor.

I blinked. One did not actually answer rhetorical questions honestly, but Miss Miller was so distressed, the truth had slipped out. She waved her handkerchief down the hall. "I went to look at the fountain in the garden through the window at the end of the corridor— the view is lovely at night with it lit up. And then I noticed a beautiful portrait of an Elizabethan gentle-woman—how uncomfortable those ruff collars must have been. How did they get them to keep their shape, do you think? Starch, I suppose." She waved the hand-kerchief to the opposite end of the hall. "And then I spotted a landscape of Parkview Hall, which must have been painted before the fountain was installed because it was just a field—so fascinating to see the changes over time. I'm afraid I lost track of time as I admired the paintings, and now I'm turned around. I don't think this is the hall I was in before." Miss Miller flourished her handkerchief at one of the window alcoves, where a panel of the drapes had been drawn back. "I can tell I'm completely turned around because when I looked out this window, the view wasn't of the gardens, but the courtyard."

"You're in the west wing." Two wings extended from the central block of the house. At the other end of the house, the conservatory stretched from the end of one wing to the other, creating an enclosed courtyard. I reached to pull the drape closed then paused, my hand on the thick fringe at the edge of the panel.

Gas lamps lined the courtyard, their dancing flames creating circles of illumination. Sonia's silhouette with her old-fashioned gown and puffy bun was unmistakable. She was speaking animatedly to someone in the shadows under the colonnade that ran along one side of the courtyard. It wasn't a casual conversation. There was an intensity to the sharp motions she made with her hands and a tension in her body. She shifted, and the light from the lamp illuminated a man's shoulder along with the glossy sheen of a dinner jacket lapel, but it didn't reach the man's face. It wasn't Father. The man wasn't tall enough. Why would Sonia meet a man in the shadowy courtyard?

Behind me, Miss Miller said, "Perhaps that nice Captain Inglebrook will come along and show us the way. It's so helpful to have a man around, isn't it? I do miss my brother Winston. He'd never have let me wander the halls and become lost. When we were houseguests he was always quite firm that I should wait for him in my room, and he'd escort me to dinner."

I drew the panel across the window and turned to Miss Miller. "Don't worry. I know the way."

"You do? How clever you must be if you can remember all the twists and turns," she said with a tone of amazement as if my knowledge of Parkview was akin to understanding physics or being fluent in Chinese.

"Not really. I practically grew up here at Parkview.

There's probably not a nook or cranny that I don't know."

"Well, isn't that marvelous."

I guided her along the corridor, past the main staircase, and said, "The drawing room is the second set of double doors on your left. You go on ahead. I have a little detour to make."

"Thank you, my dear. So kind of you. You're sure you'll be able to find your way back?"

"Yes. I'll be fine." I retraced my steps back to the main staircase. I went down to the ground floor, then along the passageway to the conservatory at the back of the house. Peter was a quiet soul and had a habit of strolling in the conservatory before dinner. I hadn't seen him for ages, and I wanted to say hello to him outside of the crush in the drawing room.

The humid warmth of the conservatory closed around me. Beyond the masses of greenery and flowering vines, the glass ceiling and walls were blackly opaque as if someone had dropped a giant cloth over the whole section of the house, cutting off the view. That thought brought Mr. Quigley to mind, and I wondered if he was sleeping in a cage covered with fabric or if Deena would bring him to the drawing room with her tonight. An earthy smell interlaced with lighter floral notes filled the air.

I wound my way through the enormous space, toward the soothing trickle of water that came from the fountain at the center of the room. The conservatory had been an excellent place to play when we were children. We'd had one game of Sardines that ended with all of us crammed together behind the ancient rubber tree and its buttressing roots that created a woody screen. The leaves of the tallest palms brushed against the glass roof while trees, shrubs, and massive urns overflowing with ferns and ivy filled the space. The aged plants created a series of screened winding paths. Green was the dominant color of the foliage, but it ranged from shades of deep emerald to paler sage to silvery olive tones.

I found Peter by the fountain in a white-painted iron chaise lounge, his feet stretched out and a cushion behind his head. Arcs of water sprayed out from the circular dish of the fountain into the shallow pool of the square lower basin, which was set into the floor and lined with colorful Italian tiles that a previous baronet had brought back from his grand tour of the continent.

Peter was smoking a cigarette as he read a book. As soon as he caught sight of me, he jumped up and stubbed out his cigarette. Unlike Gwen and Violet, who had taken after Aunt Caroline and had fair hair, Peter was dark like Uncle Leo. He came through the mix of wicker and iron chairs to greet me. "Olive, you're looking well."

"So are you," I said and meant it. His face still looked lean, but his eyes had lost their sunken look, and he seemed relaxed instead of edgy. I caught sight of the title of the book he held, his finger marking his place. "Reading up on horticulture in your spare time?"

He rubbed an eyebrow. "Farming is rather complicated."

"What are you learning about?"

"Crop rotation, animal husbandry, and bees, among other things. We have our own honey now—that's my pet project. I've been overseeing things at the home farm, and Father's given me free rein to produce and sell honey."

"That's fascinating. I can't wait to hear about it."

"Don't get me started. I can see Violet didn't warn you off. She told me if I said *honeybee* one more time, she'd scream." He crossed his arms and leaned against a chair back. "Now, what's this I hear about you and Jasper?"

"What do you hear about me and Jasper?"

"Not much. Except his voice takes on a certain tone —one that I haven't heard very often—when he speaks of you."

"That's—"

"Olive!" The shrill tone cut through the balmy atmosphere of the conservatory.

My shoulders tightened. I turned toward the sound of rustling silk. "Good evening, Sonia."

My stepmother batted a huge elephant ear leaf out of her way and crossed the black-and-white marble tiled floor to the fountain. Her gown would have been suitable for a Gibson Girl with its fitted waist, high neck, and long sleeves, but I knew Sonia wasn't wearing old gowns. She and Father were comfortable, financially speaking. They had enough to provide for themselves—and for me, if I'd chosen to live with them. I'd tried living at Tate House, but I couldn't stick it. I'd escaped to London. A poky flat—even one with damply curling wallpaper—was preferable to being under Sonia's thumb.

Sonia's mouth naturally turned downward at the corners, giving her a continual frown. "I thought I heard your voice, Olive. You do realize you're going to be late."

"I'm saying hello to Peter. I'll be along in a moment. You're fully recovered from your illness, I see."

"I'm much better." Sonia's frown deepened. "It's terribly bad manners to keep people waiting."

I clamped down on my rising irritation. "We're only a few steps away from the drawing room."

Peter tucked the book into his pocket. "Perhaps we should go now. May I escort you ladies?" He offered us his arms, and we walked on either side of him.

When we entered the drawing room, I went over to Father and Aunt Caroline, who were chatting. I'd brought down my shawl, but I wouldn't need it. Despite the size of the room with its tall ceilings and hardwood floor, it was warm with a fire crackling in the grate. The long cut-velvet drapes were drawn, keeping out the cold. More mums filled vases around the room, but these blooms were rust and orange, which blended with the muted blue and orange tones of the Axminster carpet on the parquet.

Aunt Caroline said hello, but she seemed a bit preoccupied, which was typical of her. Usually she was thinking about painting, but I knew tonight she was focused on making sure her guests were having an enjoyable evening. I gave Father a kiss on the cheek. "Hello, Father." I was delighted to see he was looking much healthier than the last time I'd seen him. His face had filled out, and he had more color in his complexion. He'd been seriously ill, and Sonia had nursed him back to health. I might have my disagreements with Sonia, but I was grateful she'd helped Father recover.

"Hello there, my dear," he said. "When did you arrive?"

"A little while ago."

"I see. I've been in the library all afternoon. I thought I might have missed you."

I patted his arm. "I'd expect nothing less from you." He and Aunt Caroline were brother and sister. While they shared few physical similarities, they both had the ability to become completely lost in whatever they were working on—Aunt Caroline in her art, and Father in his writing as he worked on a Bible commentary. "Have Uncle Leo and Mr. Payne been showing you the maps?"

"Maps?"

"Mr. Payne is here to sell Uncle Leo some maps," I said.

Father pushed up his glasses and surveyed the room, his gaze landing on Payne, who was speaking to Gwen. With her fair hair arranged in an elegant chignon and her pale pink gown bringing out the color in her cheeks, she could have been an illustration for the term *English rose*. "The overly enthusiastic chap with the adaptable face?" Father asked. "I had no idea he was here about maps. But come to think of it, he did question me closely today about whether or not I needed illustrations for the commentary." Father lowered his voice. "I'm sure he's a perfectly pleasant young man, but he simply would not stop talking. Difficult, when one is immersed in David and Goliath."

Father had been working on his commentary for years. He was only partially through the Old Testament. "You're up to First and Second Samuel, then. That's excellent." The last time I'd visited Nether Woodsmoor, he'd been writing about Joshua.

I turned to Aunt Caroline. "It's lovely to be back here at Parkview. Thank you so much for the invitation."

Aunt Caroline gave a little start. Her gaze had been fixed on Gwen, who was chatting with Miss Miller. Aunt Caroline shifted her full attention to me. "We're always delighted to have you, Olive. I didn't know if you'd be able to tear yourself away from London after all the excitement with the mummies at Mulvern House."

"The antiquities were fascinating, but I can always find time to visit you and Father." I glanced around the drawing room. "I half expected to see Deena's parrot, Mr. Quigley, here this evening. I understand she doesn't like to leave him alone."

"No parrots in the drawing room. I'm a very accom-modating hostess, but certain social boundaries should not be crossed." She drew my arm through hers as she said, "You don't mind if I borrow Olive, do you, Cecil?"

"Hmm? No, not at all. I'm just working out whether I should give a bit of background on the culture of the Philistines. Might be helpful to readers . . ."

"We'll leave you to ponder it in peace, then." Aunt Caroline guided me across the room. "Do you know what's happened between Gwen and Captain Inglebrook?"

"I've no idea. Perhaps it has something to do with Inspector Longly?" The captain had joined Gwen and Miss Miller, and he must have said something complimentary to Miss Miller because she tapped him on the arm and blushed.

Aunt Caroline frowned. "I'm still put out with Violet for sending Inspector Longly an invitation behind my back. I'm sure Violet thought it was great fun, but it's caused no end of problems."

"You wanted to invite only Captain Inglebrook?" I asked.

"Things were progressing nicely between Gwen and Captain Inglebrook in France, but since he and the inspector arrived, the atmosphere between the two men is strained, and Gwen's unhappy. Do see if you can find out what's happened. You're so good at figuring things out."

Uncle Leo joined us, and I gave him a kiss on the cheek. He handed me a drink. "I seem to remember you like this concoction called a fizz?"

Uncle Leo was a hardy man with a thick mustache. His dark eyes were surrounded by crinkles that came from squinting across the grounds of Parkview. Map collecting was his only indoor interest. On the whole, he preferred to be striding around the estate with his dogs instead of presiding over a dinner party, but he also took his duties seriously and was a good-natured host.

"Yes, thank you." I took a sip of the drink. It was

sweet with a tang of mint, which was probably fresh from the kitchen's herb garden.

Uncle Leo turned to Aunt Caroline. "I see what you're doing, Caroline. Don't send Olive out on a mission. Let her enjoy her evening." He glanced at Gwen and Inglebrook. "These young people will sort everything out on their own without any interference from us."

Aunt Caroline's lips flattened into a line. "You know as well as I do that a push is sometimes required." She was much more in favor of nudging things along in the direction she wanted them to go, while Uncle Leo had a policy of non-interference with his adult children.

"But not tonight, my dear. Leave them be."

Aunt Caroline opened a fan that dangled at her wrist and whipped it back and forth, causing the lace around her gown's neckline to flutter.

"This must be one of your gowns from Paris," I said to divert the conversation from Gwen and her suitors. As Aunt Caroline, Gwen, and Violet had made their way back from the South of France, they'd stayed over in Paris so they could order new gowns. "It's very flattering."

"Thank you, dear. We picked up a new gown for you too. I hope you like it."

"You didn't have to get me anything," I said. Aunt Caroline and Uncle Leo had always been extremely generous to me, treating me more as a daughter than a niece.

Aunt Caroline smiled. "But I wanted to. It's a deep purple velvet—aubergine. I have the village seamstress coming tomorrow to make a small last-minute alteration to my gown that I'll wear to dinner. If you'd like to wear your new gown then, I can have her make any adjustments you need." She fanned faster. "It's close in here. And Captain Inglebrook is smoking. I'll have a footman open a window to freshen things up. We can't have you coughing."

"I'm sure I'll be fine." Cigarette smoke often set off my asthma, but with the high ceilings and open space of the drawing room, the smoke would disperse. I'd only have trouble breathing if I inhaled the smoke, and I always avoided doing that.

Deena and Gigi entered the drawing room together. They were both dressed in red evening gowns. Gigi looked spectacular in a cherry red color that contrasted with her midnight black hair. Some women couldn't carry off the extremely short hairstyle of the Eton crop, but on Gigi it only emphasized her ridiculously long black lashes and her delicate features. Deena's dress was a similar bold red, but Deena didn't have Gigi's milky porcelain complexion. The bold color overpowered Deena, making her narrow face look pasty and washed-out, like a sickly Byzantine saint. Deena had gone all out with her accessories. From the ruby-encrusted combs in her hair to the tips of her red T-straps, she was completely turned out in blood red.

"Nevertheless, an open window is a good idea," Aunt Caroline said, then added, "See if you can detach Miss Miller and give Gwen a few moments with Captain Inglebrook." Aunt Caroline went to greet

Deena and Gigi, stopping to speak to Brimble, the butler, on her way across the room.

I smiled to myself. Aunt Caroline wasn't going to be deterred from her matchmaking. I wanted to speak to Gwen anyway, so I sipped my drink and made my way across the room toward them. My path took me by Peter and Longly. "How are you enjoying your stay here at Parkview, Inspector Longly?"

"Parkview Hall is an amazing estate," Longly said with a nod to Peter.

"It was certainly a wonderful place to grow up," Peter said. "We can go to the maze tomorrow, if it doesn't rain."

"When did rain ever stop us?" I asked.

"True. Olive isn't one to shrink away from the damp," Peter said to Longly.

"Gwen isn't either," I said. "We had one hide-and-seek game in the maze during a thunderstorm. Do you remember that? Gwen won."

"Of course I do," Peter said. "It's always the quiet ones you have to watch out for."

Longly smiled, but it looked as though it was an effort. Something was definitely amiss with him.

"So a visit to the maze is on the agenda for tomorrow, rain or shine," I said, then asked Longly, "Have you been working on any interesting cases?"

"It's been relatively quiet."

"Then I'm glad you could get away and join us here. I know Gwen was looking forward to seeing you."

Longly looked as if he didn't know what to say. "I'm delighted to be here," he murmured as he focused on his glass, then he tossed back the drink and excused himself to get another.

"Melancholy fellow, that one." Peter grinned at me. "I'm one to talk, I know. I've certainly had my share of bad days." He looked across the room to where Longly was standing at the drinks cart. "I'm not sure he's the best choice for Gwen, but if she likes him . . ."

"Inspector Longly doesn't seem his normal self," I said. "I wonder if his wound is bothering him—"

A bang ricocheted through the air.

Peter shouted, "Get down! Incoming!" A blow between my shoulder blades shoved me down. My knees crashed to the hardwood, and my face pressed into the fringe of the rug.

CHAPTER FOUR

"It was the draft from the window—"

"... so shocking ..."

"... frightened me, too ..."

As the jumble of words flowed around me, I pushed myself up. Peter crouched on the floor beside me. His gaze connected with mine, but no spark of recognition showed in his face. A shiver ran through me at the blankness of his stare. It was as if he looked right through me. He scanned the room, his shoulders tense, his body coiled to spring. I realized I was seeing him as he had been in the trenches—ready to fight for his life.

Sonia's whisper was loud enough to carry across the room. "... how distressing ... mortifying for Caroline . . ."

I shifted my weight off my aching kneecaps. A hand came under my elbow and helped me up. "Are you all right, Miss Belgrave?" Longly asked.

Before I could answer, Payne, who had crouched beside Peter, said in a loud voice, "It was only the door slamming, old boy. A draft, you know, from the open window. It gave me quite a scare too. Thought the Jerries were on us, for sure."

Peter blinked as he stared into Payne's face.

Payne put a hand under Peter's arm and helped him up. "Hard to let those battlefield reflexes go, I know. Guy Fawkes Night is the worst for me."

Beads of sweat had broken out along Peter's hairline. He wiped his hand over his forehead then adjusted his tie. "Terribly sorry. I don't know . . ." He turned to me. "I'm sorry, old bean. I didn't mean—it seemed so real—"

"No worries. I'm fine. Truly, I am."

A maid was already sweeping up the broken glass where my drink had shattered, and another maid was blotting the carpet.

"No harm done," I said, ignoring the throbbing in my kneecaps. Since Peter had put on a stiff upper lip and was acting as if nothing untoward had happened, I would do the same. I knew inside, he was horrified, but he was doing his best to not show any emotion.

Payne slapped Peter on the back again. "You've certainly livened things up for us this evening!"

Aunt Caroline joined us, stepping between Payne and Peter. She put a hand on Peter's arm. "Perhaps you should retire to your room . . .?"

"Of course not." Peter squared his shoulders. "If I did that, your table would be even more unbalanced." One corner of his mouth turned up in a smile. "We can't have that now, can we?"

Aunt Caroline studied his face for a moment, then she patted his arm. "Then let's go in to dinner."

I was seated between Peter and Payne at dinner. Even though Peter conversed with me and then with Miss Miller, who was on his other side, I could tell he was still shaken from the incident in the drawing room. His hands trembled as he reached for his wine, and he tensed when the footman stumbled over the edge of the rug and the spoon clattered against the soup tureen.

Payne proved to be a chatty dinner companion. I didn't like the way he'd treated Gigi earlier, but he'd been the first person to come to Peter's side tonight, and that action had raised my opinion of him somewhat.

He sprinkled his conversation with liberal mentions of his maps, but we also talked about the British Museum as well as the upcoming Egyptology exhibit that was slated to open at Mulvern House in a few months.

"I don't have any maps of Egypt," Payne said, "and that's a shame. With all this Egyptomania, I could have made a packet from something like that."

I waved off a refill of my wine as I asked, "Where do you get your maps, Mr. Payne?"

"I inherited my grandfather's collection, which is what got me started. I had no use for stacks of antique maps, but I learned collectors are keen on them. I've become something of an antique map dealer—strictly in the amateur line. I search book shops for them and travel to country homes such as this one and purchase maps from families who are either clearing things out or who are in straitened circumstances."

"I see. You must come across many interesting things."

"Oh, I do. The most popular are the signed maps." He rotated his fork. "Rudyard Kipling, Charles Dickens, that sort of thing. Those always draw the highest prices."

"Interesting. I would think those would be extremely rare."

"They are. They are indeed." Satisfaction infused his tone. He smiled at me in a way that made me think of a cat who knew it had cornered a mouse. It was an odd thought to pop into my mind, and it put me back on my guard with Payne.

Our discussion petered out there, but I'd been well-trained in the social arts and resurrected the conversation with a question. "And is this your first visit to Derbyshire?"

"No, but it's certainly a happier circumstance now than the first time I traveled here."

"Oh?"

Payne glanced beyond me to Peter, who was still turned to Miss Miller. Payne dropped his voice slightly. "I was actually here in Parkview Hall in nineteen fourteen. I was injured."

During the war, Aunt Caroline and Uncle Leo had transformed Parkview Hall into a hospital for the wounded. It had been much more of Aunt Caroline's project than Uncle Leo's. She'd put away her paints and focused solely on the hospital for two years. Uncle Leo had provided the funds, but it was Aunt Caroline who oversaw the day-to-day running of the hospital—something that went completely against her usual nature, but it was her bit for the war effort. At the end of the second year, she'd combined forces with another society matron. They decided a site in London made the most sense, both because the wounded wouldn't need to travel as far and also because the recovering soldiers could be closer to more specialized care in London. In nineteen sixteen Aunt Caroline closed the hospital at Parkview Hall and transferred her attention to Lady Marsh's London townhouse, which they transformed into another hospital.

I'd been in my early teens when the war began, and I'd pitched in at Parkview as much as Aunt Caroline would allow. Looking back, I realized she had tried to shelter me, Gwen, Peter, and Violet from the dreadful things that were happening. Aunt Caroline hadn't allowed us to spend much time with the patients. She'd had us help in other ways, like rolling bandages or knitting socks or jumpers to be sent to the soldiers.

"I had no idea," I said. "Does Aunt Caroline know you were once a patient?"

Payne's mobile face shifted into an expression of reluctance. "No, I haven't said a word. I'm sure there were so many men through here that she wouldn't remember me."

"You'd be surprised. She felt each person who came to Parkview deserved special care and attention. We've all changed in almost ten years, so you'll have to forgive her for not recognizing you immediately."

"Of course. I didn't expect her to. I wasn't here long, and . . . well, it's from a time I try not to think about." Payne's glance strayed over my shoulder to Peter.

"I understand."

"Nevertheless, I will probably join the tour tomorrow."

"The tour?"

"Of the house. Your aunt is taking everyone around who's interested. I would rather like to see my old room." He rotated his glass and stared at his wine. "Being here at Parkview wasn't like anything I imagined. We were treated like important people. There were only two of us to a room. Did you know that when I arrived, the butler wanted to know which newspaper I preferred, and if I'd have my breakfast on a tray in my room or in the dining room?" Payne shook his head as he chuckled. "Quite a change from the trenches." He watched the candlelight's reflection on the surface of the wine. "It was unreal. I felt as if I'd been transported to another world, like a fairy tale . . . or . . . a little corner of heaven."

Aunt Caroline stood and announced, "We'll be in the music room tonight. Don't linger too long in here, gentlemen. Gwen will sing for us."

She led the ladies upstairs to the music room, where a mural of Venus and Mars filled the coved ceiling. The room contained a beautiful malachite table, a few silk-covered chairs, and a satinwood harpsichord. There was space for rows of gilt-edged chairs, if Aunt Caroline wanted to host a full-scale musical evening. A piano was positioned at the opposite end of the room near the fire, and we settled around it, coffee cups in hand.

"Go ahead, dear," Aunt Caroline said to Gwen. "Run through a few songs to warm up before the men arrive."

Gwen tilted her head so that only I could see her face and widened her eyes. Aunt Caroline was doing her best to showcase her daughter's talents. I lifted my coffee in a salute of solidarity, acknowledging the pain of being the focus of matchmaking relatives. Gwen pushed back her shoulders and asked Deena, "I remember you played the piano on one of your visits. Would you like to accompany me?"

Deena stubbed out her cigarette. "Of course."

"That would be wonderful, especially if you can cover up my mistakes."

It was thoughtful of Gwen to include Deena instead of keeping the limelight for herself. As Gwen and Deena shuffled through sheet music, Gigi came to sit beside me. "Do you sing or play?" I asked her.

"Only if you want people to run screaming from the room. My talents lie in other areas," she said with a suggestive flare of her eyebrows. "You?"

"No, I have no musical talent whatsoever."

"Good, then we'll have a chat." She propped her elbow on the back of the sofa, curled her legs up on the cushion, and shifted to face me. "I must speak to you."

Gigi's serious tone wasn't like her at all. "About what?" I asked.

She drew a breath, but then Sonia sat down in a chair near us. Gigi mouthed the word *later*, then she asked me in a light tone, "What are you wearing tomorrow evening?"

"A dress Aunt Caroline picked out for me."

"From Paris? Lucky you!"

Deena played the first notes of "It Was a Dream," and Gwen launched into the song, which drew the men from their port like a siren calling to a ship at sea. Deena, her elongated faced somber with concentration as she played, stumbled over a few notes. But Gwen carried on, and Deena always recovered and found her place in the music.

Captain Inglebrook propped himself up on the arm of the sofa beside Gigi, and they held a whispered conversation. Payne smoked on the far side of the room by the window that was cracked open, while Inspector Longly stood motionless at the back of the room by the table with the coffee.

Sonia looked disapproving throughout the light-hearted verses, but Father, who'd sat down beside her, tapped his foot along with the music.

Longly, who hadn't moved an inch and had fixed his attention on Gwen throughout her songs, gave a little start when she finished and applause filled the room. He glanced around, caught my eye, and ducked his head. He sipped his coffee, made a face, and turned to refresh his cup.

Gwen bowed to her audience, then waved a hand to Deena. "And now Deena will play Mozart's 'Sonata in C Major.'"

Gwen dropped onto the cushion between me and Gigi. "Longly was transfixed," I whispered.

"What? No, he stayed as far away as he could without being impolite."

"He was so mesmerized with you that he let his coffee go cold—completely forgot to drink it."

Gwen tilted her head so she could see around me, then a deep blush suffused her cheeks. "He's staring at me."

"I don't think all hope is lost," I murmured, then gave my attention to Deena, who'd changed the music and began to play the airy notes of Mozart in a workmanlike manner.

CHAPTER FIVE

I spent most of the morning being fitted for the new dress. It was indeed gorgeous with beautiful lines. The velvet bodice was loosely fitted in the current style, but it wasn't boxy. It skimmed over my figure to a dropped waistline. The material looked almost black, but then the light caught it and brought out the deep purple tones. Because the skirt had quite a few tiny pleats, it took a long time for the seamstress to make her adjustments.

When she finished, I went down for luncheon, which was laid out in a buffet so everyone could serve themselves. I passed Mr. Payne and Captain Inglebrook coming out of the dining room.

". . . still have several excellent maps, perhaps you'd like to take a look . . ."

I was glad to avoid Payne's sales pitch, and had a nice lunch with Aunt Caroline and Deena. When we'd finished eating, Aunt Caroline said, "Will you join us on the tour of the house, Olive?"

Deena said, "No one else is coming—no other young people, I mean. It's only that map man and Miss Miller. Gigi has no interest at all. Captain Inglebrook has disappeared, and Inspector Longly has gone for a walk." Deena wore another monochromatic outfit. Her velour suit was dull rust, the most popular color this autumn, and her shoes were the same shade. I tried to imagine having enough money to have a pair of shoes that matched each outfit and failed. The extravagance of it! But Deena had come into a huge inheritance a few years ago. She could probably afford to change her shoes every hour if she wanted.

"Of course I'll join you." I knew Parkview Hall well and could probably have given the tour myself, but when one is a houseguest, one always participates in suggested activities if one is invited.

Payne was standing in the entry hall waiting for us, his hands in his pockets as he walked back and forth across the checkerboard marble floor.

"Mr. Payne," Aunt Caroline said, "so glad you could join us."

"Yes, certainly." His gaze scanned our group, and I suspected he was considering whether he could gracefully make his excuses because he didn't want to be the only gentleman, but he fell into step behind Aunt Caroline as she moved around the entry hall, pointing out details about the ceiling mural, the Roman busts, and the refurbishment of the staircase in the last decade.

After we'd made a circuit around the room, Aunt Caroline said, "You've all seen the dining room, the sitting room, and the drawing room, so we'll focus on some of the other areas of the house." Her heels clicked across the marble to one of my favorite places at Parkview. "But first, the library. I know Mr. Payne"—Aunt Caroline dipped her head toward him—"is already familiar with this room."

He said, "It's one of the finest libraries I've had the pleasure of browsing."

"How kind of you to say that. We do enjoy it. I'm sure you're familiar with the maps my husband collects, but we also have some nice first editions he probably didn't even mention."

Aunt Caroline pushed open the door, and I wasn't surprised to see Father settled in a wingback chair near the fire with not one, but four books open on his lap and balanced on the arms of the chair. Sonia sat in the matching chair with a piece of needlework.

Father began closing books so he could stand when we came into the room, but Aunt Caroline waved him back to his seat. "No need to get up. We're simply passing through—a little tour of the house."

Aunt Caroline walked us through the library, pointing out various rare books. "The second baronet was a bookworm and oversaw the construction of the gallery," she said as she gestured to the second story that ran around the entire room.

Deena ran her hand along the rail of the circular staircase that twisted up to the gallery. "Oh, may I go up?"

"Yes, of course," Aunt Caroline said as Payne drifted over to Sonia and Father.

"What a cozy domestic scene," Payne said as he rocked on his heels, hands in his pockets.

Father looked up from his books, "Hmm? I'm sorry, did you say something, Mr. Payne?"

"Nothing of importance, dear," Sonia said to Father, her needle flashing back and forth through the fabric.

Payne moved back to join our group, a little smile on his face that looked . . . I searched for the right word . . . *gleeful.*

Deena tugged at my sleeve. "Olive, we're moving on."

"Oh, right. Sorry." I fell into step with her. We toured the billiard room, stopped briefly in the music room, then went on to the portrait gallery.

Mr. Payne paused on the threshold and murmured, "Ah, *this* I remember. It was the activities room."

Aunt Caroline had her arm raised to a portrait of a man on horseback. She was about to launch into a story about the third baronet, but her arm dropped. "Mr. Payne, were you here during the war?"

"I confess I was, Lady Caroline. Only for a short time in nineteen fourteen. I must say, staying at Parkview Hall was one of the few bright spots during those years." He rotated, taking in the whole room. He nodded toward one of the long windows. "The dominos were over there. Further along the wall were the tables with jigsaw puzzles." He rocked on his heels and nodded. "Yes, this was indeed a respite."

"I'm glad to hear it," Aunt Caroline said. "We strove to have a peaceful atmosphere that encouraged healing."

"You achieved your goal in my case." He tapped his left leg. "My broken leg healed up nicely. No problems with it at all."

"Excellent," Aunt Caroline said. "Wonderful! It was always touch-and-go with broken legs."

Payne's mobile face had shifted into a serious expression. "You have my sincerest gratitude for all you did at that time."

"Thank you, Mr. Payne, but I must say it was a cadre of people who made the hospital a success. Beyond the hardworking doctors and nurses, everyone for miles around pitched in and did their bit to help. You might want to revisit the library. We have a collection of photographs from that time. Gwen used her Brownie camera to document the changes to the house and to photograph the staff and patients. The photos are in albums on the bottom shelf of the bookcase nearest the circular staircase."

"Thank you, Lady Caroline. I'll do that," Payne said.

We moved on and viewed some of the guest rooms that weren't currently occupied. When we reached the mahogany room, Mr. Payne hesitated on the threshold, then slowly stepped inside the room. "Yes, this was where I stayed. I wondered if I'd recognize it. My bed was on the far side over there, and there was another here, near the door." He walked to the window that looked out over the courtyard, then turned and came back. "It even smells the same. That earthy, herby scent takes me back."

"It's the chrysanthemums. We always have them at this time of year in all the rooms," Aunt Caroline said as she prepared to move on to the next room. Deena hadn't come into the room and still lingered in the doorway. She stepped back hastily as Aunt Caroline came through. Aunt Caroline turned back. "You may stay longer if you like, Mr. Payne."

He gave a small start. "No. Sorry. Lost in thought."

Payne hung back from us during the rest of the tour. We could barely draw Miss Miller away from the china room and Parkview's extensive collection of Wedgwood and other porcelain.

We finished the tour in the conservatory with Aunt Caroline pointing out the rubber tree with its long buttressing roots as well as the banana tree and pineapple plants. Deena and I trailed along after Miss Miller, who stayed beside Aunt Caroline, asking questions about the plants, particularly about the rare orchids that had been brought back when a Victorian baronet sponsored a plant hunting expedition to the tropics.

We returned to the fountain, where Payne waited. He'd been sitting in a wicker chair, smoking a cigarette. He threw it into the fountain and stood when we rejoined him.

Deena said to Aunt Caroline, "May I bring Mr. Quigley in here? He would absolutely adore it."

Aunt Caroline blinked. "Mr. Quigley?"

"My parrot."

"Ah, yes. Er—I suppose that would be fine. Just not in the mornings when Ross is tending to the plants or before dinner. That's when Peter likes to stroll in here. It would give him a fright if a parrot landed on his shoulder."

"Mr. Quigley's very well mannered," Deena said. "He'd never do that."

"I'm sure he is," Aunt Caroline said without a trace of conviction in her tone.

Gigi sailed into the conservatory. "Good, I found you. We're about to leave for the maze. Who wants to come?"

Aunt Caroline glanced at the glass ceiling. Beads of moisture dotted the exterior of the glassing, blurring the view. "It's terribly drizzly and cold."

"We'll bundle up," Gigi said. "Don't worry about us."

"Then I'll have a nice fire going for you in the drawing room along with hot drinks when you come back," Aunt Caroline said.

"Sounds lovely." Gigi took my arm and Deena's and walked us to the entry hall, where Brimble and several footmen were waiting with our coats. Payne made his excuses and peeled off from our group, heading for the library.

Captain Inglebrook said to Gwen, "You look smashing in that velvet hat. Paris, I believe?"

Gwen murmured her thanks while Inspector Longly stood a little to one side, his face somber, but he wore a coat and hat, so he was also going with us. Longly nodded to us while Inglebrook greeted each one of us in turn.

Inglebrook was bundled up as well, but he'd added a white silk scarf to his overcoat, which only enhanced his resemblance to a film star. He spoke to everyone, but he lingered by Gigi. She linked her arm through his. "Shall we go?"

We set out through the gardens, which were muted and rather plain at this time of year. The misty air, which was tinged with the aroma of wood smoke, felt good after the stuffiness of the rooms. We left the formal gardens and tramped through soggy leaves along the path that took us up over the hill and around the lake to the maze. I slowed, dropping back so I could fall into step beside Longly, who was bringing up the rear of the group. I said, "I thought you'd already been for a walk today."

"One can never have enough country walks," he said as he watched Gwen, who was striding along a few steps ahead of us beside Gigi and Captain Inglebrook. I tried to maneuver the group so Gwen and Longly could walk beside each other. I'm sure Aunt Caroline could have performed the shuffling of people with ease, but I wasn't able to achieve it before we reached the maze.

Gigi eyed the eight-foot-tall shrubbery. "Excellent. It's even taller than you, Captain Inglebrook, so you can't cheat."

"You think *I* would cheat?" He pressed a hand to his chest, wrinkling the silk scarf.

"Undoubtedly. Catch me if you can." Gigi darted through the gap in the hedge that was the entrance. Inglebrook took off after her.

Gwen said to the rest of us, "There's a fountain in the middle. See you there. Good luck."

She shot a quick look from under her lashes at

Longly, but he was adjusting his coat and missed it. Gwen ducked her head and entered the maze. I hung back, chatting with Deena, and was happy to see Longly follow only a few steps behind Gwen.

Deena and I wandered about the maze for a while, but then we separated. She wanted to go left, and I knew the right-hand turn was the correct direction. As I worked my way to the center, I turned a corner and discovered Inglebrook had indeed caught Gigi. They were in a dead end of the maze, kissing. It wasn't a quick peck on the lips either. Their arms were wrapped tightly around each other, and even though I walked on quietly, I didn't need to worry about being stealthy. They were lost in their own world.

I reached the fountain a few moments after Deena, who arrived first. She clapped her hands. "Is there a prize?"

"Only bragging rights."

Deena's lips puckered into a pout. "Oh well."

The rest of the group trailed in, Inglebrook with a smile on his face and Gigi adjusting her cloche. I was happy to see Longly and Gwen stroll in side by side. Their hands were tucked into their pockets, but their steps were perfectly synchronized. They continued to walk together all the way back to the house, pausing only when Longly's empty sleeve caught on a branch and pulled free of the pins that held it against his jacket. As I passed them, Gwen said, "Here, let me," and folded the sleeve back into place. The look Longly gave her as she bent her head to refasten the pins made me think he wished they were in a secluded corner of the maze instead of out in the open. Since Gigi and Ingle-brook were still paired up, I walked beside Deena, who gave me an exhaustive primer on parrots.

We gathered in the drawing room for tea, and Deena and I took a seat by the fire near Miss Miller and Sonia. Payne rejoined us and sat across from us, sipping his tea.

We told him about the maze, and Deena tilted up her chin. "I got to the fountain first."

"Congratulations," Payne said, his tone dry. He put down his cup. "I think I'll move. The heat from the fire is quite suffocating."

"We could change seats," I offered, but he declined and moved across the room.

Aunt Caroline sat down near us. "I've received a note from Jasper. He's had trouble with his motor. He says he'll do his best to arrive before dinner this evening. I do hope he makes it. I don't want another dinner with thirteen."

"So unlucky," Miss Miller agreed as the dressing gong sounded.

When we walked out of the room, Payne was waiting in the hall. "A moment of your time, please, Miss Miller," he said.

It seemed an odd pairing. Payne had sought out the company of the younger women, like Gigi and Gwen, despite being nearly a decade older. I couldn't remember any time that he'd singled out the older women like Miss Miller or Aunt Caroline. Well, that wasn't quite true. He'd spoken to Sonia in the library today, but it still seemed odd that he'd want to speak to

Miss Miller. I looked back at the pair a few times as I went down the hall to my room. After a moment, Payne stopped speaking, and Miss Miller gave a nod. I didn't go into my room until Payne walked away.

The seamstress had finished my dress, and it was spread on my bed. After I bathed, Hannah kept up a running commentary on the beautiful construction of the dress and options for accessories. As the gown swished over my shoulders, I said, "Just the pearls, I think."

She twitched the hem into place and handed the necklace to me. "So lovely, those pearls. Now shall I brush your hair?" With my bobbed hair, there wasn't much Hannah could do to arrange it, other than smooth it into place and add a decorative clip. I put on a little bit of lipstick and rouge, then went down for dinner, hoping Jasper had arrived.

I was at the door to the drawing room when a sharp clacking sound, shoes striking quickly against the marble, reverberated up from the entry hall. Deena came flying up the main staircase, a long royal-blue feather in her hair fluttering as she ran. She jerked to a stop, and her dangling diamond earrings swayed back and forth. She snatched my hands. "He's not moving." She pulled me down the stairs, her earrings slapping against her cheeks as she spoke over her shoulder. "Oh, do hurry. It's awful."

CHAPTER SIX

I struggled to keep my feet under me as Deena dragged me down the stairs. "Deena! Slow down. What's happened?"

The sequins on her dress sparkled with the rapid rise and fall of her chest. "I don't know what happened. He was just *there*. He looks"—she let out a shuddery breath—"I think, I mean—I don't know—I didn't stay to look. But he's gray and not moving. I think he might be dead."

My heart thumped, and I felt lightheaded. "Peter?" He was always in the conservatory at this time of day.

Deena clamped a hand on my wrist. "This way." Her royal-blue skirt fluttered around her legs and batted against me as she towed me toward the conservatory. "I went in to have a peek, to see if anyone was around," she said. "I thought I might be able to bring Mr. Quigley down and let him fly around for a few moments if no one was in there. I never thought—it was such a shock, seeing him there on the ground."

The conservatory's steamy atmosphere enveloped us, and Deena released my wrist. She took the lead, scurrying along the path through the banks of greenery, her pale blue shoes flashing against the black-and-white tiles as she ran. I dashed along in her wake, dodging under banana leaves and batting away the trailing ivy that caught at me.

Movement flickered in the corner of my eye, a flash of something light colored, a pale purple. No, it was mauve. The paleness of the color contrasted with the shades of green. I only got a glimpse of it through the dense greenery, but I could tell it was a fabric with a sheen—perhaps silk?

"Olive! Why did you stop? Over here." Deena motioned for me to catch up with her, then ran around the last twist of the path and into the open area around the fountain.

A man in black tie was lying on his back, his head on the decorative tiles that lined the rim of the fountain's lower pool. Another man bent over him, his back turned to us.

I let out a breath. The man stretched out on the ground wasn't Peter. His hair was too light. It was Mr. Payne. My legs went wobbly as relief flooded through me.

I moved past Deena, who'd jerked to a stop at the edge of the path where it opened to the central area. Within a few paces, I could see the hunched figure was Peter—evening dress made the men look so similar, especially from the back. He knelt beside Payne, his hand at the man's collar.

I knelt beside Peter. The stiff surface of Payne's boiled shirt wasn't moving. His eyes were open, but they had a dull veneer that meant he'd never blink again. Shock rippled through me at the sight. I couldn't see any visible injury on Payne, but the tiles around his head were spotted with red drops. And then I saw the back of his head was quite damaged. I swallowed and looked away, concentrating on the area around the fountain as I composed myself.

Dirt from an overturned pot sprinkled across the floor. Here and there, footprints—some partial and some complete—crushed the dark crumbles of earth, while two lines cut through the sweep of the granules, running in a faint semicircle from the pot to Mr. Payne's heels.

"What happened?" I didn't look at Payne again, but focused on Peter. The skin around his left eye was swollen and red. "Gracious, Peter, your eye!"

He didn't seem to take in my words.

"Were you in a fight? Did someone hit you?" I asked, glancing at Payne, but Peter didn't reply, and my stomach flipped. He didn't seem to see me at all. If I'd stood up and walked away, I doubt he'd have known I was there. His expression was vacant and far away. I touched his shoulder. "Peter, it's me."

He blinked and focused on my face. "Olive?"

"Yes. It's Olive." A flare of fear raced through me— this was horrible, just horrible. I tried to quash my emotions as I fought to keep my tone even. "What's happened?" I asked, striving for the same tone I'd have used to ask, "Care for a game of tennis?"

I looked down at Payne. Peter's gaze followed mine. I still had a hand on his shoulder and felt the shiver run through his body.

"I don't know." He turned back to me. His words were jerky, and he seemed confused. "He was just—lying here—like this."

I tugged on Peter's shoulder. "I don't think there's anything we can do. But we should send for Sonia."

"Yes. Right." Peter stood and backed away, his gaze still fixed on Payne. The color washed out of Peter's face, and his fingers trembled as he reached up to touch his bruised eye. He didn't look steady on his feet, so I took him by the elbow and guided him to the grouping of wicker chairs, which were tumbled over. I set a chair upright and pushed Peter into it, pressing his shoulders forward so he was bent over with his head near his knees.

I turned to Deena, who had inched closer to the fountain. "Find Sonia," I said. "My stepmother, Mrs. Belgrave. She has nursing experience."

Deena nodded and ran across the trail of dirt.

I called out, "And Inspector Longly." Deena jerked back toward me, her face puzzled. "Go," I said. "Hurry."

She nodded and scuttled away, stepping around a chaise lounge that was on its side. She brushed by a trailing ivy vine, and it waved in her wake.

I knelt in front of Peter so that my gaze was on the level of his. "Peter, what happened?" I felt quivery, but I fought to hide my own turmoil and keep my tone smooth.

Peter, still in his hunched position, raised his head. His hair, usually slicked back, had fallen forward in straggly clumps from his hair tonic. The stiff surface of his shirt and his evening suit were smeared with dirt. He looked at me—really looked at me—and I could tell he was seeing me and not some distant haunting vision from his past. "I don't know." His tone was low, and his words were hesitant as if he were picking through hazy memories. "I came in through the door from the west wing." He tilted his head toward the far end of the conservatory, where Deena had just left.

"I don't remember much after that. I must have come along the path through the plants there." His brow crinkled, and he winced, then touched the corner of his eye, which was swelling. "I think I tripped over a chair."

I swiveled on my heels and looked carefully at the area around the fountain. Most of the chairs and tables were overturned. Fragments of wicker and chair cushions were scattered across the floor. The iron chaise that Deena had stepped around was directly in the path of someone entering from the west wing, and Peter's book about beekeeping lay near it, splayed open, facedown with the pages wrinkled.

Deena's continuous babble of words sounded and grew louder along with the swish of silk. I grasped the arm of Peter's chair to steady myself as I stood, but Peter caught my hand and helped me up as he rose with me. "I know I'm a bit off at times." He touched his forehead. "But I had nothing to do with . . ." He nodded to Payne's body.

I squeezed his arm and released it as Sonia entered the central open area, going straight to Peter as she said, "Now what's all this?" in that jolly artificial tone that nurses and nannies tend to use. Apparently, Deena hadn't explained the situation clearly, and Sonia thought Peter was having another of his "episodes."

I nodded to the fountain. "It's Mr. Payne. I don't think there's anything we can do for him."

Sonia pivoted toward the fountain and froze for a moment.

I said, "I sent for you because you have nursing experience . . ."

"Yes, of course." Her voice had a distracted quality. She knelt beside Payne, checked for a pulse, then brushed a strand of hair away from his forehead in a gentle gesture that surprised me.

I'd always thought Sonia would be a fearsome nurse, someone who by the sheer force of her personality would convince—or demand—that her patients recover, but perhaps she showed more compassion to her patients than she did to people in her daily life. Perhaps that was the secret of her nursing success.

She sat back on her heels. "There's nothing we can do." She checked her watch and murmured, "Half past seven," a holdover from her nursing days, I was sure.

My throat constricted, and Peter dropped his head and stared at the floor. Deena, who'd had the fingers of both hands pressed to her lips, now fisted her hands together at her throat. "How ghastly. Was it an accident? What happened?" She turned to Peter, but he didn't move or say anything.

"Excuse me, Miss Lacey." Inspector Longly stepped around Deena, who shifted away as if someone had pointed a hot poker at her. Longly scanned the scene around the fountain, his gaze resting for a long moment on Payne, then he raised his eyebrows at Sonia.

She shook her head. Longly nodded, then his voice assumed an authority that I hadn't heard from him since I'd arrived at Parkview. "Right. If you could all step into the drawing room, I think that would be best. Miss Belgrave, perhaps you could summon Brimble and have him contact the local authorities."

"Apologies for interrupting your evening plans," Inspector Longly said. He stood in the drawing room, his feet planted on the center of the vine-patterned Axminster carpet while the rest of us ranged around the large room. Instead of the usual pleasant, low hum of chitchat punctuated with laughter, the room had been tense and quiet while we waited for the inspector. The only sounds had been an occasional muted murmur and the crackle from the blaze in the large fireplace.

Peter stood at the far end of the room. He'd drawn back one panel of the drapes and stared out into the garden, his back turned to the group. I imagined he wished he could escape outdoors. He was like Uncle Leo and would rather be outside, but that wasn't possible tonight. Aunt Caroline had exclaimed over his black eye and sent for ice, but the cold compress dangled from his hand at his side.

Aunt Caroline, sapphires sparkling at her ears and throat, pulled her gaze away from Peter. "It's certainly not your fault that you've been put in charge here, Inspector. Poor Mr. Payne. Such a sad situation. What can you tell us about it?"

"Not much at the moment, I'm afraid. I'll be able to give you a clearer picture later." He looked to Uncle Leo. "The local authorities have asked me to take charge of the investigation. With your permission, Sir Leo, I'd like to speak with each guest individually tonight. The chief constable will join me as I interview everyone."

"Of course." Uncle Leo stood behind Aunt Caroline, who was seated in one of the plush velvet-covered chairs. The lines in his face looked deeper, and his attention also kept straying to Peter. "I'm sure everyone will cooperate fully." He put a hand on Aunt Caroline's shoulder. "Caroline and I would be happy to speak with you first."

"Yes, certainly." Aunt Caroline reached for her shawl as she prepared to stand.

Longly said, "Thank you, Sir Leo."

Captain Inglebrook leaned forward. "It must have been an accident, Lucas."

It took me a moment to realize the captain addressed Inspector Longly by his first name. Up until that moment, I'd almost forgotten Inglebrook and Longly were childhood friends. I hadn't seen them spend much time together, and they had such different personalities.

Inglebrook sat on one of the sofas between Deena

and Gigi. His evening wear was spotless, and his dark hair was combed back from his face, every hair in place. Gigi lounged in one corner of the sofa, blowing smoke rings at the ceiling in a leisurely manner, but Deena started when Inglebrook spoke. The feather in her hair bobbed and her diamond earrings swung as she jerked toward him. Her jumpiness was understandable after what she'd seen in the conservatory. I was still on edge too.

Inglebrook went on, "The chap must have tripped and cracked his head. I don't see what all the fuss is about."

Obviously, he hadn't seen Payne's head. A fall couldn't have caused that much . . . damage. I shut down that train of thought as Inglebrook smoothed a hand along his thin mustache and continued, "Surely we can dine, Lucas, then you can ask your questions later."

Longly said, "It's too early to make any statements regarding Mr. Payne's death."

I glanced from one man to the other. They might have been childhood friends, but there was definitely a rift between them now, and I didn't think it could be put down completely to a rivalry for Gwen's affection. Inglebrook had been much more attentive to Gigi.

In a fluid movement that reminded me of a cat, Gigi stood, and the simple lines of her bright pink sheath dress fell into place. Her only jewelry was a narrow band of seed pearls that she wore across her forehead and threaded through her dark hair. "Then you won't need to speak to me—or Captain Inglebrook. We didn't see Mr. Payne after tea. Captain Inglebrook and I played billiards until it was time to dress for dinner."

"On the contrary, Lady Gina, I need to speak to each one of you to create a full picture of everyone's movements this evening." Longly's voice was heavy with a note of authority.

Across the room, Gwen's pale gold gown blended with the cream upholstery of her chair. She'd been fiddling with the clasp on her topaz bracelet. She snapped it closed. "But you won't need to speak with Peter straightaway, Inspector. That can wait until tomorrow, can't it? He's had a terrible shock. Surely you understand."

"I agree, it's a difficult time, but I've found it's best to talk with everyone immediately, when impressions are fresh. If Mr. Stone can spare me a few moments, I'd like to speak with him tonight."

Peter turned from the window. My stomach clenched at the sight of his eye, which was now swollen closed. He gave Gwen a warning glance as she drew a breath to continue her argument. Peter said to Longly, "I'd be happy to talk with you at your convenience."

"Thank you," Longly said and turned to Sir Leo. "Despite your generous offer to talk with me first, Sir Leo, I'd like to begin with anyone who was in the conservatory this evening. I believe that includes Mr. Stone," Longly said with a nod to Peter, then turned to me, "and Miss Belgrave."

"Certainly," I said, already running through what I'd say, feeling a twist of fear as I remembered the strange look in Peter's eyes. I'd stick to the facts, I decided. I'd state exactly what happened, nothing more —no embellishment or elaboration.

Longly looked to Sonia. "As well as Mrs. Belgrave."

Sonia and Father were behind me. The cameo Sonia wore at the throat of her high-necked gown bounced as she swallowed. "Of course," she said in a blank yet deferential tone that I'm sure she'd often used when she'd said, "Yes, doctor."

She stood a little behind Father. He drew her arm through his, pulling her to his side. Sonia leaned against him, and I realized that Payne's death had probably brought back difficult memories for her too. She must have seen awful things during the war.

Longly pivoted back to the sofa. Gigi had dropped onto the arm and now sat swinging one delicate foot back and forth. She'd always been fidgety. Sitting in a classroom in boarding school had been torturous for her, but she stilled her movements as Longly's gaze swept over the sofa to the opposite end. "And I must speak to Miss Lacey as well."

Deena's head jerked up. "Me? Surely, you don't need to talk to me. I was only in the conservatory a minute or two. I just peeked in, really."

"It's vital I speak to you, Miss Lacey. You found Mr. Payne."

"But Peter was there too."

"You raised the alarm," he amended. "We'll get into all that in a moment." Longly glanced around the room. "Was anyone else in the conservatory between tea and the time Mr. Payne's body was discovered?"

I looked at Miss Miller, who was seated in an

armchair near the fire, the skirt of her mauve silk gown ballooning around her chair. She twisted her handkerchief around one finger, unwound it, and then wrapped it around another finger. She didn't say a word.

Longly turned to Uncle Leo. "If we might use your library . . ."

At Uncle Leo's nod, Longly said to Peter, "Mr. Stone, if you would be good enough to accompany me to the library, we'll begin with you."

CHAPTER SEVEN

*I*nspector Longly looked up from his notebook and said to me, "You described Mr. Stone as hunched over Mr. Payne's body with his hands at Mr. Payne's throat, is that correct?"

We were seated on opposite sides of the large reading table in the library. A constable sat at the far end, scribbling in his notebook. Colonel Havens, the local chief constable, was in a nearby armchair, the smoke from his pipe drifting to the ceiling.

"Yes," I said. "That was where Peter was when I first saw him, but he wasn't in a threatening pose."

Colonel Havens took his pipe from his mouth. "How could you tell?"

"Peter was searching for a pulse." Of course that was what he was doing. I stopped myself before I mentioned Peter's blank gaze and confused state. Longly had said nothing directly to indicate he suspected Peter was involved in Payne's death, but his detailed questions made me nervous for Peter.

Longly looked back at a previous page of his notes. "And he didn't say anything to you when you arrived?"

"No."

"But you spoke to him?"

"Yes, I said we should send for Sonia, and he agreed." I pushed the thought of Peter's mute state out of my mind.

"And you asked him what had happened?"

"Correct. As I told you earlier." We'd been through these details before, along with questions about Payne's friends, family, and business, which I couldn't tell Longly a thing about, except that Payne sold maps. I clamped down on my impatience with Longly's thoroughness. I was anxious for the questioning to end before I slipped up and said something that might make Longly more suspicious of Peter.

"And what did Mr. Stone say?"

"He thought he'd tripped over the chaise lounge."

Longly pounced on the word. "Thought?"

The cold finger of worry traced along my spine. "I don't remember exactly what he said word for word."

"I see."

To derail his line of questioning, I asked, "What about the dirt?"

Longly's pencil paused. "Dirt?"

"There were two faint lines in the dirt on the floor. They ran from the overturned pot to Mr. Payne's heels, but when Deena went to fetch Sonia, she smudged them. Were any traces of the lines left?"

"The conservatory is currently being documented

with photographs and drawings." His tone indicated the subject of the dirt on the floor was closed. Longly flipped to a new page in the notebook. "And what was Mr. Stone's mental state?"

The cold grip of fear squeezed my heart. It was the question I'd been afraid would come up, and I didn't want to answer it. "What do you mean?"

"How did Mr. Stone seem? Was he confused? Muddled?"

"In his right mind, you mean?"

My tone was sharp, and Longly put down his pencil and rubbed his shoulder on the side of his evening suit with the empty sleeve. "I know this is difficult, Miss Belgrave. But these questions have to be asked—especially after the incident in the drawing room yesterday."

I pushed back my chair. "Then I suggest you find somebody who is an expert in these things to answer your questions. All I know is that Peter was checking for a pulse, and Mr. Payne was clearly dead when I arrived."

"Olive, old bean," a voice called. I was halfway across the entry hall and hadn't noticed the figure at the door handing his overcoat, top hat, and cane to Brimble. Jasper came across the black-and-white tiles, his long legs moving at his usual unhurried stride, his fair curls rumpled from his hat and untamed by hair tonic. "I had a spot of bother with the motor and left it in Upper Benning for repairs."

"Jasper, thank goodness you're here." I crossed the room to him, hands outstretched. Before I thought about it, I pressed myself to his chest. After a second, his arms closed around me.

His voice was low and soft as he said in a completely different tone, "What's all this? Don't get me wrong—I find it an enchanting welcome, but this is not the normal reception I receive, even when I'm rescuing a hostess from serving dinner to thirteen guests."

I pushed back from him. "I'm sorry. I forgot myself for a moment. But I'm so glad you're here. Something terrible has happened. Mr. Payne is dead, and Inspector Longly suspects Peter did it."

All trace of humor drained from Jasper's face. "Peter?"

"Yes, because of an incident in the drawing room last night. A window was opened, and the draft caused the door to slam. Peter reacted as if he were back in the trenches. It was quite frightening and—well, at the time we just thought it was embarrassing, but now, with Mr. Payne's death and Peter's black eye . . ." I stopped and drew in a deep breath. "I'm making a hash of all this. Come with me to . . . um . . . the music room. It should be deserted. I'll tell you everything."

Jasper followed me into the music room, and I said, "You'd better close the door. I don't think anyone should overhear this."

The sound of our heels tapping across the hardwood floor echoed around the empty room. It was a contrast from the prior evening when the room had been filled with music and applause.

I sat down on a backless settee with scroll arms, and Jasper drew an armchair over. As I summarized what had happened, Jasper listened with his elbow propped on the chair's arm, his chin resting on his hand and his fingers curled against his mouth.

When I finished, he pulled his hand away from his face. "You think Peter did it."

I bristled at his astonished tone. "I'm *afraid* he did it. I don't want to believe he did it. Oh, if you'd seen his face—that glazed look. I'm sure he was confused and—and—muddled, is the only way to describe it. He didn't know what had happened."

"He didn't do it," Jasper said. "There are boundaries that he wouldn't—couldn't—cross."

"But what if something set Peter off, like the crash of the door in the drawing room last evening? He was completely immersed in those awful memories, acting them out among us. My knees still ache from when he slammed me to the ground." All my worries came pouring out. "I don't think Peter would intentionally harm Mr. Payne. Of course I don't. But perhaps Peter was in the middle of one of his . . . episodes. If he thought he was on the battlefield . . ."

Jasper shook his head. "I can assure you Peter would never do anything like that." Jasper's normal temperament was rather lighthearted. He didn't take life too seriously, but he was more somber now than I'd ever seen him.

I leaned forward. "Then how did Peter get his black eye? He and Mr. Payne must have fought—"

"Tell me about Mr. Payne."

"All right," I said, glad to move away from the subject of Peter's mental state. "Mr. Vincent Payne. Where to begin?"

"With that face you just made, I suspect there was something unsavory about the chap."

"He was an odd mix. He became too—well, he overstepped with Gigi. She slapped him."

"Gigi always could take care of herself."

"True. But Gigi's rebuff didn't seem to faze Mr. Payne. I mean, he did look upset, but only for a short time. He was contrite and apologized, then he acted as if nothing had happened," I said, thinking of the way Mr. Payne had held out his arm, ready to walk with Gigi back to Parkview. "A little later, he was mingling in the drawing room—although, he did give Gigi a wide berth."

"I'll bet he did. Maps, you said? Sir Leo must have been interested in those."

"Of course. In fact, that's the reason Uncle Leo invited Mr. Payne to Parkview. Uncle Leo wanted to buy maps from him."

"So Mr. Payne sold antique maps?"

"Yes, but he wasn't a dealer, I gathered. More something he dabbled in on the side. Although Mr. Payne was forceful about them."

"Hmm . . . map dealers rarely turn up dead in suspicious circumstances, I believe."

"I know."

Jasper leaned forward and rested his elbows on his knees. "Now, what's this about dirt that you mentioned earlier?"

I explained about the overturned pot and the soil scattered across the floor in more detail. "There was a swath of dirt." I flattened my hand and swept it in an arc. "The odd thing was that there were two parallel lines in the dirt that ended at Mr. Payne's heels, but Deena went out that way to find Sonia and they came back the same way, so their footsteps obliterated most of the lines."

"But it looked as if Mr. Payne's heels had been pulled through the dirt over to the fountain?"

"Exactly," I said. Thinking about the positioning of Mr. Payne's body, I added, "His limbs were aligned, with his legs straight and arms lying by his side."

"Which probably wouldn't be the case if he'd fallen," Jasper said.

"It doesn't seem likely, no." I frowned. "Captain Inglebrook assumed Mr. Payne's death was an accident, that he'd fallen and hit his head—Deena must have told him what she'd seen in the conservatory—but it does seem as if Mr. Payne was attacked, then dragged over to the fountain and arranged so it appeared as if he'd fallen backward into the rim and hit his head, but his head looked—"

"Quite," Jasper said quickly. "You don't have to describe it again. You went rather white the first time. If someone moved Mr. Payne's body, that's hardly the reaction of someone in the midst of an episode of shell shock, which should be a point in Peter's favor, assuming Inspector Longly thinks Peter was caught up in some sort of delusion. Peter wouldn't drag Mr. Payne to the fountain. That's the action of someone trying to obfuscate the truth. If Peter were muddled and confused, he'd be in no state to think as clearly as that."

"Perhaps Peter thought Mr. Payne was an injured man on the battlefield," I said, hating to even put my thoughts into words. "Maybe Peter thought he was dragging him back to safety?"

"And then posed Mr. Payne with his head balanced on the rim of the fountain?" Jasper shook his head. "No, it sounds far too lucid, especially if Peter was in the grip of a war neurosis. Perhaps Peter simply walked into the conservatory and saw the dead body, which gave him a bad turn."

"Then how did he get his black eye?" I asked. It was another question I didn't want to dwell on, but we couldn't ignore it. Longly certainly wouldn't.

"You said Peter thinks he tripped at some point," Jasper said. "Perhaps Peter came into the conservatory, caught sight of Mr. Payne, and didn't see the over-turned chaise lounge."

When Jasper said the words *caught sight*, something pinged in my mind. "Oh! The mauve fabric!"

"Mauve fabric?"

"Someone else was in the conservatory. When I followed Deena in, I caught a glimpse of mauve-colored fabric through the greenery. I couldn't see anything else, but there was a definite mauve fabric showing through a small gap between the plants."

Jasper said, "The conservatory does have several paths. Someone could have taken the one that curves around the outer edge of the room and wraps back to the doors."

"Only one person was wearing mauve tonight— Miss Miller."

"Refresh my memory. Who is Miss Miller again?" Jasper asked. "I know you mentioned her in your earlier synopsis of the situation, but I don't remember what you said about her."

"That's because there's not much to tell. She's a spinster, one of Aunt Caroline's bridge partners. She kept house for her brother, but he recently passed away. She's flighty and tends to ramble on."

"Hmm . . . no reason to attack Mr. Payne?"

"None that I can think of. And she seems frail. I'm not sure she could do . . . something like that. But when Longly listed the people he wanted to speak to first, those who'd been in the conservatory this evening, she didn't say a word. I meant to tell him earlier, but it completely went out of my head when I spoke to him in the library because I was so worried about Peter. I should tell Inspector Longly immediately. Perhaps Miss Miller saw something that will clear Peter."

"Why didn't she speak up straightaway?"

I sighed. "I don't know. I hope it was because she didn't want to become involved in a police investigation. Gently bred ladies avoid things like that." Jasper grinned, and I cut him off before he could make a comment. "I, on the other hand, am a special case. I must involve myself in these situations. My work requires it."

"And you're curious."

I grinned back at him. "That, too."

Jasper stood and extended a hand, pulling me up. "I hope you're right and Miss Miller can help clear up what happened. I'm off to find Peter and have a chat." He squeezed my hand before he released it. "Don't worry. We'll sort this out."

We met Brimble in the entry hall. "A cold dinner buffet has been laid out in the dining room," he said.

"Thank you, Brimble," I said. "Perhaps later."

"Is Peter in the dining room?" Jasper asked Brimble.

"No, sir. I believe he's retired to his room for the evening."

Jasper thanked Brimble, then said to me, "Let's meet later. Perhaps in the billiard room?"

"I don't think I'll be up for a game of billiards."

"No, to compare notes. That's how this sleuthing bit works, correct?" He gave me a quick smile and strode off down the corridor, at a much quicker pace than his usual saunter.

I didn't go into the dining room. Since I was a working girl, I tended to take advantage of every lavish meal I possibly could. Any break from my threepenny buns and tepid tea was welcome, but I wouldn't be able to eat tonight. My stomach felt too queasy.

I tapped on the open library door. I must have caught Inspector Longly between interviews because he was alone. "Miss Belgrave, please come in."

"I won't take up much of your time, Inspector. I wanted to mention something I forgot to tell you earlier."

Longly gestured to the seat across the table from him and reached for his notebook as I told him about seeing the mauve color in the conservatory.

"Mauve? Could it have been a flower or vine of some sort?"

"No. It was fabric. It had a sheen like silk."

Longly's gaze tracked back and forth across the surface of the table, and I thought he was probably mentally reviewing everyone's evening attire.

"Only one person wore mauve tonight—Miss Miller. I hate to be a tattletale, but I felt I had to mention it."

He consulted his notebook, turning back the pages. "Miss Miller says she rested in her room after tea then went straight down to the drawing room before dinner." He made a note. "I'll speak with her tomorrow. She's retired for the evening. Thank you, Miss Belgrave."

CHAPTER EIGHT

I moved along the hallway, reading the name cards beside each door. Longly had to wait until tomorrow to speak to Miss Miller. It would be bad form to request to speak to her after she'd retired for the night. He might be a detective inspector, but summoning an elderly guest from bed just wasn't done. However, I was a fellow guest and might be able to chat with her if she was still awake.

Down the corridor, a maid came out of one of the rooms, pulled the door closed, and walked away from me. The same door opened, and Miss Miller leaned out with her back turned to me as she called the maid back. Miss Miller was in a dressing gown, and her fair hair was woven into a long braid that hung down her back.

I hurried forward so that I could speak to her before she disappeared back into the room. I reached her door just as Miss Miller held out a pair of cream-colored shoes to the maid. "These need to be cleaned."

The maid reached for the shoes, which had a black

smudge on one of the toes. "I'm sorry, miss. I'll see to it right away."

As Miss Miller handed the shoes to the maid, she tilted them, exposing the soles. Bits of deep black dirt—the same shade as the potting soil that had been spilled on the conservatory floor—were ground into the soles of the shoes.

"Wait a moment," I called to the maid, who'd half-turned away, and she halted.

Miss Miller spun around. I reached for the shoes and turned the soles upward. "You were in the conservatory this evening, weren't you, Miss Miller?"

Her face went as white as the lace on her dressing gown. She swayed. I caught one of her arms, and the maid caught the other before Miss Miller crumpled.

I stumbled back, holding her up. Worry washed over me. Was Miss Miller in bad health? I shouldn't have let my question burst out like that. She wasn't faking a *spell*, as some ladies did. Miss Miller was a dead weight. "Help me get her to the bed," I said to the maid.

The maid and I got her to the bed, and I sent the maid for smelling salts. I arranged a blanket over Miss Miller, and my concern receded a bit because she was breathing easily, and her color was coming back to normal. I bent down and collected the shoes the maid had dropped when she helped me catch Miss Miller. I put them on a chair at one side of the room, then returned to the bed, where the maid was waving smelling salts under Miss Miller's nose.

She gasped and opened her eyes, then waved her

hand. "My handkerchief. I need my handkerchief." The maid handed her a freshly laundered one from a drawer, and Miss Miller wiped her eyes and nose, then lay back against the cushions. "I'm sorry," she said to me. "My vision went all spotty. I suppose I shouldn't have skipped the cold buffet dinner, but I couldn't stomach any food tonight."

I turned to the maid. "Fetch Miss Miller a cup of tea and perhaps some dry toast."

"Yes, miss." The maid curtsied and left the room.

I drew the chair from the dressing table over to the bed and sat down. "You'll feel better once you have some tea and toast."

"I shouldn't have taken the sleeping draught on an empty stomach. That never goes well," Miss Miller said in a distracted tone.

"I apologize. I shouldn't have made such an abrupt statement. I didn't mean to shock you."

Miss Miller's gaze had begun to dart about the room while I spoke. She spotted the shoes on the chair and lunged forward to grip my hand. The quick movement surprised me. Her thin fingers were cold and strong as they clamped down on mine. "I didn't know what to do this evening when Inspector Longly asked who else had been in the conservatory—it's so sordid to be involved in a police investigation. Winston would *not* have approved."

I patted her hand in what I hoped was a reassuring manner. "It's not pleasant, but you must tell Inspector Longly."

"Oh, I don't think I could. And I'm sure what I have

to say isn't important. I was only in the conservatory for a moment. It would be so embarrassing to confess that now. I didn't even plan to go into the conservatory at all, but I saw that horrible Mr. Payne go in, and I—" She released my hand and picked up the handkerchief. She twisted it around her index finger and then unwound it.

I massaged my fingers. "But you did eventually go to the conservatory, didn't you? Otherwise, you wouldn't have dirt on your shoes."

She rewound the handkerchief as she sighed. "Yes, but how I wish I hadn't. This would all be so much simpler if I'd gone on into the drawing room instead. If only Mr. Payne had never sold his maps to Winston."

Talking to Miss Miller was a bit like trying to catch a butterfly. Her mind darted around, and it was hard to follow her, but I felt as if we were getting to the heart of the matter. "Mr. Payne sold your brother a map?"

"Several maps. And they were all fakes."

"Oh my."

"Well, not the maps themselves. They *were* antique maps. It was the signatures on the backs that were forgeries. Winston was so swept up in his excitement at owning maps signed by Rudyard Kipling and Charles Darwin that he snapped them up—along with several others. It was only after Winston passed on and I was having his things valued—because what use are antique maps to me?—that I learned the signatures were all forgeries."

She smoothed out the handkerchief on top of the blanket. "When I met Mr. Payne here, I recognized him immediately. Of course he didn't remember me at all. I was only the spinster who poured his tea and arranged his dinners when he stayed with us." She plucked at the lace on the handkerchief. "But I didn't want Sir Leo to be taken in by that—that—*schemer*. He's a conman, you know. I mean, he *was* a conman."

She'd gotten worked up, but now she fell back against the pillows. "It was *such* an embarrassing situation. You saw what Mr. Payne was like, how persistent and persuasive he was. If I went to Sir Leo and told him Mr. Payne sold Winston forgeries, I was sure that Mr. Payne would pooh-pooh my words and convince Sir Leo I was mistaken. I decided to tell that nice Captain Inglebrook about it yesterday. I explained everything to him. He said he'd have a word with Mr. Payne. And he must have, because Mr. Payne came to me this afternoon."

She pressed herself deeper into the pillows. "It wasn't a good idea, asking Captain Inglebrook to handle it. How I wish I could go back and change that as well. I should have left well enough alone." She paused as she yawned. Then she gave her head a little shake and worked herself up higher against the cushions so she sat up straighter. "This afternoon Mr. Payne came and said—well, he said he knew something about me that I wouldn't want to get out."

"Knew something about you?" What secret could this fluttery woman have?

Miss Miller leaned forward and lowered her voice. "My surname isn't Miller. It's Muller—a German name."

"Oh, I see."

She went back to plucking at the lace on her handkerchief. "When the war started, my brother decided it would be best if we became the Millers. He'd retired from his job in the city, and we were moving to Nether Woodsmoor, where we weren't known. Winston said changing our name was the prudent thing to do. You remember how much the Germans were reviled, don't you?" she asked. "Still are reviled."

"Yes, I understand." I didn't like to think someone would treat Miss Miller differently because of her surname, but I knew it was true.

She became more animated as her eyes narrowed. "But then after Captain Inglebrook warned him off, that awful Mr. Payne pinched my letter. An old one from this very room—a letter I'd saved and cherished. It was from my sweetheart. He died in an accident in eighteen ninety. It was addressed to Miss Marion Muller, and it was one of my most precious possessions. He had no right to search through my belongings," she added in a rush, her cheeks flushing pink. "Mr. Payne had the nerve to say that if I didn't keep quiet about the maps he'd sold to Winston, he'd make a point of 'finding' the letter during tea and reading it aloud so everyone would know my true last name."

"What a bounder."

Her burst of energy faded quickly. She stifled another yawn and nodded behind her hand. "I—well, I'm sorry to say I was a coward, and I told Mr. Payne I'd inform Captain Inglebrook it had all been a mistake, which I did. But then this evening when I saw Mr. Payne go to the conservatory, I thought perhaps I could convince him to give the letter back. He hadn't said anything about returning it. I should have made him promise to give it back before I agreed to what he wanted. I did *so* want that letter."

"So you went into the conservatory . . ."

"I did, but only after walking back and forth for a few minutes in the corridor. I decided I really must do it. I plucked up my courage and rushed in. I didn't see Mr. Payne or hear him moving about. I decided he must have left, so I wound my way through the paths—it's so easy to get turned around in all that vegetation, isn't it? But eventually I followed one of the paths to the fountain. I thought I'd take a moment and admire the lily pads—such a beautiful and unusual flower! In fact, there are so many unique flowers in the conservatory—"

"What happened when you got to the fountain?" I asked, anxious to keep Miss Miller from going off on a tangent.

She drew in a breath and pressed her hand to her chest. "I was shocked—so *shocked!* Mr. Payne was lying there on the ground, motionless, and his eyes—" She shivered. "It was truly dreadful." She picked up the handkerchief and wound it around her index finger. "But then I thought that might be my only chance. If he had the letter with him at that moment, I could get it back. I knew from one look that Mr. Payne was gone. I did my bit during the war, keeping the men company and writing letters for them. One poor man died while I was reading to him from *The Thirty-Nine Steps*, just slipped away." She lifted her free hand and wiggled her fingers, wafting them through the air, a sketch of his departing spirit. "And then there was Winston. I was there with him, holding his hand when he passed on, so I know what death looks like."

I didn't interrupt her this time. Her face was sorrowful as she paused, lost in memories. Then she drew in a breath and returned to the present. "Mr. Payne's death meant there would be police and questions that I didn't want to answer, so I"—she swallowed—"forced myself to check his pockets."

She unspooled the fabric from her finger. "The letter was in his tailcoat pocket—thankfully, that section of his coat wasn't under his body. I could reach it without touching him. I found my letter. It was only as I stood up and turned away that I saw poor Mr. Stone. He was over near the other path, not the one I'd come down."

My hope that her story would clear Peter, which had been inching up as she spoke, plummeted.

"Seeing him gave me even more of a fright." Miss Miller pressed her hand to her chest. "I hadn't realized he was there. A large overturned pot had hidden him from my view. I was so frightened. *Two* dead men! But then Mr. Stone twitched, just his foot. He groaned, too, so I knew he was alive. I scurried past Mr. Stone—I did feel terrible leaving him—but I was afraid someone might find me there."

"So, you didn't see anyone else in the conservatory?"

"No. I fled."

"And earlier, when you were walking along the path

through the conservatory, did you see anyone? Even a glimpse?"

"No." Another yawn caused her jaw to crack. "Excuse me. I'm so drowsy—the sleeping draught, you know."

I suppressed a frustrated sigh. Miss Miller must have left shortly before Deena checked to see if the conservatory was empty. If only Miss Miller had arrived a little earlier, she might have seen what happened. Her story wouldn't help Peter—if it was the truth. I searched her face, trying to work out if there was any guile in her sleepy blue eyes. She blinked and cranked her eyebrows up in an effort to stay awake.

"So, you have the letter now?" I asked.

She pulled a wrinkled envelope with faded handwriting from her dressing gown pocket. "I'm not letting it out of my sight now."

"I imagine not." It wasn't proof, but it did verify a portion of her story because I could see the handwriting. The envelope was addressed to *Miss Marion Muller*. "I realize the whole incident is distressing, but you must tell all of this to the inspector. It's much better for him to hear it from you than to find out you were in the conservatory and kept it from him." As disappointed as I was that her story wouldn't help Peter, her presence in the conservatory was part of the puzzle of what happened, and Longly needed to know about it.

She snuggled down into the pillows. "I suppose I must," she agreed, her tone similar to a child who knew they had no choice in a matter, "but I'll do it tomorrow."

I wondered if it was the sleeping draught making her compliant or if she'd really changed her mind.

The maid returned, and Miss Miller stashed her letter under a pillow. The maid set a tray across her lap, then departed. Miss Miller struggled up a few inches. "I'll just nibble on this and then get some rest. I'll have a word with the inspector tomorrow."

"I think that's a good idea."

"Perhaps . . . you could be with me when I speak to him?"

"I'd be happy to."

Miss Miller ate a few birdlike bites of toast, sipped the tea, then settled back on the pillows, her eyelids drooping. I removed the tray, tucked the blanket around her shoulders, and rang for the maid. Once she'd taken the tray, I picked up the cream-colored shoes and tiptoed from the room. I hoped Miss Miller wouldn't change her mind about speaking to Longly, but I decided I'd take charge of the shoes just in case.

I checked the billiard room to see if Jasper was waiting for me there, but it was empty. So much for comparing notes on our sleuthing. I went down to the ground floor. It appeared everyone had followed Miss Miller's lead and retired early. Most of the rooms were dark and silent. The hallway leading to the conservatory was blocked off with a row of chairs. Down the dim corridor, I could see the door to the conservatory was closed and probably locked as well, I imagined. The library and the drawing room were deserted.

I climbed the stairs to my room, wondering if Jasper had retired early as well or if he was still with Peter. I wasn't about to go knocking on his door or Peter's after everyone had retired. That would be highly inappropriate. I'd have something to tell Jasper over breakfast—or lunch, I supposed. Jasper was not an early riser.

As I opened the door to my room, a voice came from inside. "Finally! Where have you been?"

CHAPTER NINE

*H*and pressed to my heart, I closed the door. "Sonia, you frightened me half to death."

In one corner of the room, a single table lamp was switched on, its glow illuminating the birds and flowers on the wallpaper. Sonia, still in her evening gown, stood in front of the light. She picked up a book from the table. "I've been waiting for nearly half an hour. I told your father I was going to pick a book from the library. He'll wonder what's become of me. Where have you been?"

"Speaking to Miss Miller."

"Oh." She hadn't expected that answer. She probably thought I'd been holed up in Gigi's room looking at magazines while Gigi smoked cigarettes. "Well, I only wanted to speak to you for a moment." Sonia squeezed the book. "You must find out who killed Mr. Payne. Do"— she circled a hand in the air—"whatever it is you do, and make sure it's cleared up. For Peter's sake."

I was still carrying Miss Miller's shoes. I put them down on the bureau and went across the room. "What's brought about this change? I thought you disapproved of me working."

"*Disapprove* is a strong word. I simply think you should act in a manner that befits your station. However"—her tone lost its condescending note and became brisk as she clutched the book with both hands—"if you can help the family avoid scandal, then you have an obligation to do that."

"Of course. I'll do whatever I can to help Peter."

"Good." Her stranglehold on the book tightened, and she seemed to be about to say something more, but she only said, "Good night," and swept past me as she left the room.

"Well, that was odd," I murmured. I didn't ring for Hannah to help me out of my gown. I went behind the lacquered screen and changed into the night clothes and dressing gown that Hannah had laid out for me.

A tap sounded on my door. A deep voice whispered, "Olive?"

I belted my dressing gown and opened the door an inch, then stepped back and swung it wide. "Jasper! You look a little worse for wear."

He was leaning against the doorframe, his arm braced on it with his head resting on his forearm. "I am."

Jasper was usually impeccably groomed, but some substance smeared one of the lapels of his tailcoat. His hair, which was never tidily smoothed down, was even more disheveled than usual. A heavy aroma of cigarette smoke emanated from the tailcoat. Jasper did smoke—not usually around me because smoke bothered me—but he never reeked of it.

"Where have you been?" I sounded much like Sonia's usually snappish tone, so I added, "I looked for you in the billiard room."

"I've been at the White Duck Pub in the village." He enunciated each word carefully.

"Jasper, you're squiffy!" I'd never seen Jasper drink to excess.

"Afraid so."

"Then we'd better talk in the morning."

"Ah, but you'll want to know the important news I picked up this evening—it concerns our case."

"Our case?"

"The murder of Mr. Payne—quite a catchy ring to that. It would make a good book title, don't you think?"

I looked around Jasper. Thankfully, the hall was empty. "You'd better come in." I didn't want Sonia to find Jasper in this state outside my door in case she came out of her room on her way to the bath.

"Only for a moment." He heaved himself off the doorframe, ambled in, then propped himself up against the dressing table. He waved a hand at me. "You stay over there. You smell far too good for me to be responsible for my actions while I'm in this state if you get much closer. Roses with a touch of gardenias, I think."

I had put on a floral scent that evening. I felt my cheeks grow warm. Jasper had flirted with me before, but tonight his light teasing veneer was thinner than usual, and his gaze had an intensity that I found . . . intriguing, I realized with a start. I decided it would be best to ignore the comment—and the funny flutter of my heart. "So, why have you been downing pints at the pub?"

"All in a day's work, old bean. After I made sure Peter wasn't about to do something foolish, I chatted with one of the police chaps—"

"What do you mean, do something foolish? Is he . . . distraught? He seemed to be—well, not fine, but at least not too overwrought when I saw him in the drawing room."

"My dear girl, the general consensus is that he lost his head and killed a man. Of course he's distraught. Fortunately, Lady Caroline convinced him to drink a cup of tea, which contained a sedative. It's one that he's been prescribed but usually refuses to take. It's probably the best thing for him at the moment. He'll sleep straight through to morning."

"I hope the rest helps him. Perhaps tomorrow he'll remember more of what happened in the conservatory."

"One can hope, but I'm not waiting around for that. Memories are fickle. I'm following your example and searching out answers."

"How unusual of you."

"I know. But this involves Peter. When I was a sniveling, lonely eight-year-old fresh off the ship from India, he rescued me from a life of shuttling between dotty aunts, which is truly a fate worse than death for a young boy."

It wasn't like Jasper to even mention the past or become sentimental. I was tempted to see if I could prod him into further disclosures, but he frowned at the carpet. "I seem to have wandered away from my point. What was it?"

"Something about the police."

His head popped up, and he gripped the dressing table as he took a deep breath. "Mustn't do that," he said in an aside. "Yes. Right. I learned from one of the police lads that Dr. Grimshaw is the police surgeon who examined Mr. Payne's body. I also discovered the good doctor frequents the White Duck every time he visits Nether Woodsmoor, so I went down to the village."

"Clever."

Jasper had picked up one of the bottles on the dressing table. He fell silent as he rotated the scent bottle, gazing at the facets.

"And I assume Dr. Grimshaw was at the pub?" I asked, otherwise it might take until dawn for Jasper to recount his evening.

"What? Oh—yes." Jasper replaced the bottle and turned to me, but he moved his head at the same pace as the turtles we'd watched at the river when we were children. "Dr. Grimshaw can put away his pints. I bought him a round—or five—perhaps more? I lost track. A few careful questions revealed all. Mr. Payne was indeed murdered."

I sat down in the armchair, a feeling of dread settling

over me. It wasn't surprising news, not after I'd seen the state of Payne's head, but it was still unnerving to know Longly's inquiry was now officially a murder investigation.

Jasper crossed his arms. "Someone beaned the poor chap near the crown of his head. So that washes out Captain Inglebrook's theory of an accidental fall. If Mr. Payne had fallen backward, the injury would be lower on the head, nearer the back of the skull, not the top. The doctor said it wouldn't be possible for someone to fall from a standing position and strike the crown of their head on the rim of the fountain. 'It was all wrong,' he said." Jasper paused.

Furrows formed in his forehead. "There was something else . . . oh yes! The shape of the wound. I'll spare you the rather gruesome bits, which Dr. Grimshaw gave me in great detail. The upshot of it is that Mr. Payne was struck with something that has a shallow concave shape. Dr. Grimshaw said the police found several garden spades that would fit the bill in the storage cupboard at the back of the conservatory. They've taken them off for examination."

"So it's as we thought. Someone struck Mr. Payne on the head, then dragged him to the fountain in the hope that it would be assumed an accident. Such a disturbing thought." Knowing another person, a medical authority —even a drunk medical authority—agreed with our assessment made the situation more distressing than when we'd been speculating about what had happened.

"Seems that way, doesn't it?"

"But what does that mean for Peter? Did the doctor

have any thoughts on that? Did he agree that if Peter was in the midst of reliving some sort of memory that he was on the battlefield, he wouldn't do something like that? It's too elaborate, isn't it?"

"I couldn't pin Dr. Grimshaw down to anything specific on that topic, but the chatter at the pub tonight was all about how awful it was that young Peter had cracked up and killed someone. Even the good doctor said it was regretful."

I straightened, shifting forward to the edge of the chair. "That's horrid. How could the villagers say that? They've known Peter all his life."

Jasper levered himself off the edge of the table and put a hand on my shoulder. "Don't worry. We'll put it all to rights—tomorrow. Thankfully, you have some experience in this sort of thing. Now I must toddle back to my room, or else I'll curl up here on your floor and fall asleep like a faithful hound." Jasper wove his way to the door, which he had trouble opening. "Now, when did they add those extra doorknobs? Must cause no end of confusion."

"I think you'll find it's all much clearer in the morning." I reached around him and opened the door. After a quick check that the corridor was deserted, I asked, "Do you think you're all right to make it to your room?"

"Oh yes. Just down the hall—no worries. Grigsby will be there to scold me about the stickiness on my tail-coat and tuck me in, tutting like Nanny. Good night, fair Olive."

He paused for a moment and swayed toward me,

his face rapt as he looked into my eyes. My pulse did a lively foxtrot as his gaze dropped to my lips, and I realized I wanted to lift my chin and lean toward him. He drew back sharply and let out a shuddery breath as he turned away.

I watched him for a moment as he made his unsteady way down the hall in a serpentine path, weaving toward the massive medieval tapestry that hung on the wall, then redirecting his steps. I thought he was going to collide with the glass-fronted antiquities cabinet, but he straightened his course at the last moment, and only his shoulder grazed it. Otherwise, he made it to his room without incident.

I closed my door, took a deep breath to calm my heartbeat, and realized I hadn't even told Jasper about my conversation with Miss Miller. It was probably better that I hadn't. He might not have remembered it. I'd tell him in the morning.

I sat down at the dressing table and creamed my face, my thoughts on Jasper. I'd had a pash for him years ago, but we were friends now—good friends—chums, even. But the way he'd looked at me . . . I blew out another breath. That was so much more than a friendly look. I picked up my comb. What would I have done if he'd kissed me? Would I have kissed him back? We'd come to such a nice place. He was the only person I trusted implicitly. Did I want to risk losing that?

Oh, why was I even pondering this? In the morning Jasper probably wouldn't even remember that little tug I'd felt between us. It was only a typical male reaction to the scent of roses and a woman in her dressing gown.

I screwed the lid onto the cold cream and climbed into bed, determinedly turning my thoughts away from Jasper and focusing on Payne instead. Who hated him so much?

CHAPTER TEN

*T*he first thing I noticed when I walked into the breakfast room the next morning was Mr. Quigley the parrot perched on the back of Deena's chair. I did a quick survey of the room for Aunt Caroline, but she wasn't present, thank goodness. I was sure she wouldn't appreciate a houseguest bringing a bird into the breakfast room.

Deena saw my hesitation and waved her fork over her shoulder. "Don't worry. Mr. Quigley is very well behaved. He doesn't like to be closed up in the room all day alone, and the conservatory is still blocked off. They're searching for evidence, I suppose."

I filled my plate and returned to the table.

Deena picked up her toast. "I do hope the police chaps hurry. It's most inconvenient to not have access to the conservatory." She pitched her voice higher. "Does Mr. Quigley want some bread?" She broke off a corner of the toast and offered it to the parrot.

He made a trilling sound and announced, "I am the

bread of life," then plucked the food from Deena's fingers.

Deena twisted in her chair. "Mr. Quigley! You can talk! You naughty bird. You've been holding out on me. What else can you say?"

Mr. Quigley inched sideways across the back of Deena's chair. Deena swiveled around, following the bird's progress as he transferred to the other side of the chair back. She held out another tidbit of bread. Mr. Quigley snapped it up, then flitted to the top of the hutch. Deena returned her attention to her plate, cutting into her kippers. "What a funny thing to say."

"You did say he was owned by a missionary, didn't you?" I asked.

Deena tilted her head. "Yes, but I don't see what that has to do with it."

Father, who'd been filling his plate at the sideboard, turned to her. "The reference is John six thirty-five. 'I am the bread of life. He that cometh to me shall never hunger; and he that believeth on me shall never thirst.'"

"Oh," Deena said. "How . . . um, clever of Mr. Quigley." She looked less than delighted with the parrot's skill. "Well, perhaps he knows other things too, like quotes or poetry."

Father sat down beside me. "Yes, maybe something from the Psalms."

Deena said, "Er—yes."

Father leaned toward me as he reached for his flatware and said in a low voice, "Although, I don't think it's appropriate to make light of the Scripture."

"I think it's better than Mr. Quigley coming out with salty language."

Father considered, then dipped his head in acknowledgment. "That's true. The Word doesn't return void." He paused, shook his head, and buttered his toast. "However, I can't say I've heard of a parrot spreading the Good News. Always a first time, I suppose."

Jasper sat at the far end of the table, sipping a milky yellow concoction. With his careful movements and dark circles under his eyes, he almost looked worse than Peter, who was beside him. Peter lifted his black coffee and sipped from it every few minutes in a rote sort of way. The skin around his eye was beginning to turn blue and deep purple, and his shoulders were tense. He stared at his coffee cup in an unseeing way that indicated his thoughts were far from the breakfast room.

Mr. Quigley squawked, and the crystal in the chandelier trembled. Jasper winced and put a hand to his temple.

Gwen was on my other side. She didn't even jump at Mr. Quigley's sharp call. All her attention was focused across the table on Peter. "You'd feel better if you ate something," she said to him. Gwen was ignoring her own advice as she moved eggs around her plate.

"I doubt it." Peter finished his coffee. "Time for me to make my rounds."

Gwen set up straighter. "Where are you going?"

"I need to check the bees, and then I have to discuss repairs to some of the farm equipment with the men."

Gwen put down her fork. "You can't go on with your day as if nothing happened."

"That's exactly what I have to do." Peter pushed back his chair. "It's the only way I've been able to get on since the war, old thing. Can't change now."

Gwen looked from him to Jasper, clearly hoping Jasper would intercept Peter, but Jasper was downing the rest of his odd-colored drink in several swift gulps. Peter paused at Gwen's chair on his way around the table. He didn't say anything, just squeezed her shoulder then moved on.

Inspector Longly entered the breakfast room just before Peter reached the door. "Good morning, Mr. Stone. I need to speak with you."

"Certainly."

"Thank you. One moment." Longly addressed the room, "Good morning, ladies and gentlemen." Everyone stopped eating and turned to Longly. "I know some of you planned to depart either tomorrow or Monday, but everyone must stay here for the time being —except, of course, Mr. and Mrs. Belgrave," Longly said with a nod in Father's direction. "Returning to your home in Nether Woodsmoor would be accept-able." His gaze swept the room. "Everyone else needs to remain here. Sir Leo and Lady Caroline have graciously agreed to extend their hospitality a few more days. I apologize for any inconvenience."

Longly turned back to Peter, and I looked at Gwen. She'd be the one coordinating food and seeing to the guests if we all stayed on for an extended time, but her gaze was fixed on Peter.

Longly had drawn him to the side of the room, but his quiet words were still audible as he said to Peter, "Would you be so kind as to accompany me to the police station in the village?"

The clink of flatware against china had resumed, but it stopped again.

Peter squared his shoulders and gave a nod. "Of course." I thought it was probably the same type of response he'd have given to a commanding officer during the war. He was obeying an order, not fulfilling a request.

Gwen stood, her chair rocking at her abrupt movement. I steadied it as she said, "There's no need for Peter to go down to the police station. Surely you can ask your questions here at Parkview?"

Longly turned, his posture stiff as he answered Gwen. "I'm afraid it's not at my discretion. The superintendent insists."

What an awkward situation for Longly—a houseguest put in charge of investigating his hosts. I wouldn't be surprised if someone was sent to replace him soon. Or perhaps the superintendent was taking charge now.

Gwen must have missed the miserable look in Longly's eyes because she fisted her hands. "Surely you can convince the superintendent that's not necessary."

"I've tried. He's adamant."

I pushed back my chair and moved around the table. Gwen rarely became angry, but if someone she loved was threatened, she was rather like a mother bear protecting her cubs. I wanted to intercede before things escalated between her and Longly. "Inspector, if I could have a moment of your time?"

"I'm afraid—"

"I assure you it's important. I wouldn't interrupt you otherwise." I lowered my voice. "It concerns a person who was in the conservatory last night but was afraid to speak up about it."

Longly had been watching Gwen out of the corner of his eye, but that statement drew his attention. He turned fully to me. "Indeed?"

I gestured to the hallway. "Perhaps I could tell you a bit more?"

I'd stopped by Miss Miller's room on my way down to breakfast and found her bright-eyed and munching away on a piece of toast heavy with marmalade. I'd reminded her of her promise to speak to the inspector, and she'd sighed. "Yes, I can see now that I've calmed down that it's something that must be done—like taking a horrible tonic when one has a cough. Best get it over with as soon as possible."

Longly glanced at Peter, then said to me, "Yes, I suppose I'd better see to this now." He turned to Peter. "I suggest you remain here at Parkview this morning."

Peter gave a little half bow. "I await your summons."

Longly followed me down the hall to one of the window alcoves, which was bright with morning sunlight. The clouds and drizzle were gone, but it was chilly despite the sunshine. I crossed my arms as the coolness penetrated the tall panes of glass. I relayed to Inspector Longly what Miss Miller had told me the evening before, concluding with, "I convinced Miss Miller it would be in her best interest to speak to you this morning and inform you of her presence in the conservatory. She'd like me to be with her when she speaks to you."

"Back to your meddling ways, I see." Out of the breakfast room and away from the tension between Peter and Gwen, Longly had relaxed slightly. He almost looked like his old self, and although I didn't like the insinuation that I was interfering, I was glad to see him less anxious.

"I can't help it if people tell me things," I said.

"Interesting how often that occurs."

"Perhaps if people weren't afraid of speaking with you, they might not confide in me."

"Am I that fearsome?" His gaze strayed back to the breakfast room as Gwen came out of the doorway. Her eyes narrowed as she stared at Longly, then she turned and marched away.

"Gwen is fiercely loyal," I said. "She's trying to protect Peter."

"I understand that. But I must do my job." The tension in his posture was back. "Perhaps you could summon Miss Miller and meet me in the library."

"Thank you for telling me what happened, Miss Miller." Inspector Longly closed his notebook and gave a nod to the sergeant, who'd sat at the far end of the table, writing down everything Miss Miller said.

Miss Miller watched the sergeant depart, then said, "I do hope you're able to keep information of such a delicate nature . . . quiet."

It was a good thing Miss Miller had brought a fresh handkerchief to the interview. She'd given the delicate fabric quite a working over, twisting, turning, and crumpling it as she answered Longly's questions.

"I'll do my best to make sure it's not shared, and I'll see your letter is returned to you as soon as possible," Longly said as he tucked Miss Miller's letter into the pocket of his suit jacket. When Miss Miller had told him she'd retrieved the letter from Payne's body, the inspector had asked to see it. Miss Miller had hesitated a moment, then taken it out of her dress pocket, saying, "I thought I should keep it with me."

I'd had to do very little during the interview. My only role in the proceedings had been to sit beside Miss Miller and nod encouragingly at critical points.

As the envelope disappeared into Longly's pocket, Miss Miller crushed her handkerchief into a clump. "Oh, must you keep it?"

"I promise I'll return it to you at the first possible moment."

His sincere tone must have convinced her he'd keep his word. "Thank you, Inspector. I do appreciate it. And if you could do so in private? It could be so embarrassing—"

"Yes. Right. Well, I don't want to keep you from the rest of your day."

I hid a smile. Longly was adept at interviewing people. He'd managed to curtail many of Miss Miller's ramblings and kept her to the point, which I considered an achievement.

Longly's words were a dismissal of me as well. We all stood, and as Miss Miller and I left, Longly had already turned to the sergeant who'd been taking notes at the far end of the table. "Sir Leo said yesterday that he purchased three maps from Mr. Payne. Let's request to see those . . ."

Outside the library, Miss Miller and I paused. She patted my hand. "Thank you, dear. It wasn't nearly as ghastly as I feared. Now, Lady Caroline is expecting me to play a few rounds of bridge this morning. I believe Miss Stone and Miss Lacey will be there. Will you join us?"

I couldn't sit at a card table. I'd be a poor partner. I had too much on my mind. "No, thank you. You go ahead." I wondered how Aunt Caroline could concentrate on bridge, but she was an excellent hostess and would make sure her guests were entertained despite a police investigation going on around her.

As Miss Miller went on her way, I considered where I might find Jasper. He would have finished breakfast by now. He was probably in the billiard room. With its wood paneling, it was nice and dark, a perfect location for someone recovering from a hangover on a brilliantly sunny day. The sergeant returned, darting by me into the library, his face tinged with excitement. I lingered outside the open library doors.

His animated voice carried. "Inspector, I think you'll want to see Mr. Payne's room. Once the lads finished in the conservatory, they moved to the victim's bedchamber, and it's a right mess, it is. Someone's tossed it."

"What? I locked that room last night myself," Longly said, his words growing louder at the end of the sentence.

I scooted away from the door and was on the lowest steps of the staircase seconds later when Longly and the sergeant passed me with quick nods, their feet beating out a fast tattoo as they trotted up the stairs. I drifted along in their wake until they came to the green room, which had been Payne's.

Inspector Longly stood just inside the threshold, his hand braced on his hip. "It certainly didn't look like this last evening."

I hovered a few steps away, but I could see around him. The guest room with emerald-colored damask silk walls was a mess.

The contents of the wardrobe and every drawer had been tossed on the ground. Some of the room's paintings tilted at odd angles, while others lay on the floor. The Hepplewhite desk chair had been overturned, and the bed was stripped of its sheets and blankets. Two police constables were moving around the room, examining the items that covered the floor.

The sergeant gestured to the door. "The lock must have been picked, sir. The door was shut but unlocked when they arrived."

Longly asked, "Have they found the maps?"

"No, sir."

"Sir Leo said he bought three of the six maps Mr. Payne showed him," Longly said. "I'd expect to find the remaining three here, but no trace of them, you say?"

"None. In fact, they've found nothing interesting at all. Only Mr. Payne's personal belongings—clothes and a shaving kit—and that envelope." He gestured to a white envelope, likely taken from the writing paper stocked in the desk from the look of the heavy paper. "That one there, under the desk. No one's touched it yet."

Longly took a single glove from his pocket and braced it against his hip as he worked his hand into it with a practiced motion before he picked up the envelope.

The envelope wasn't sealed. He opened the single sheet of paper it contained. "Looks like it's Mr. Payne's copy of the invoice for the maps he sold to Sir Leo." Longly returned the paper to the envelope and put it on the desk. "We'll need to take the envelope into evidence, Sergeant."

"Right, sir," the sergeant said, then added, "The constable took the liberty, sir, of asking Lady Caroline if anything was missing. She sent her daughter, Miss Stone, who said none of the room's contents had been taken. She couldn't vouch for Mr. Payne's things."

Longly put his glove away, then ran his hand over his mouth and chin as he surveyed the room. "Did you check the top of the wardrobe?"

"Yes, sir. It's bare."

"And between the mattress and box spring?"

"Yes, sir. Nothing unexpected. Same situation with the drawers and under the rugs."

I stepped forward. "Have you checked the cupboard behind the wainscoting?"

The inspector and the sergeant turned to me. Before Longly could send me on my way, I said, "There's a recessed cabinet. The previous Lady Stone had them installed for storage when the bedrooms were renovated, but no one really uses them. Well, except for Peter, Gwen, and me. They were excellent hiding places for our loot when we were children."

Longly waved his hand. "Please, show us."

I crossed the room and knelt by the wall near an armchair. "It's cleverly done. The trim of the wainscoting hides the door seam—well, except for this little bit at the bottom. Unless you look closely, you wouldn't know there's a cabinet here at all. You press the corner of the wainscoting here—" The panel popped open an inch, and I pulled it back. "I believe this is what you're looking for." The cabinet contained a thick tube of paper about two feet long. The bottom of the cabinet was dusty, but the roll of paper wasn't.

"Blimey," the sergeant said. "How would Mr. Payne know about that hiding place?"

I nodded to the nearby armchair. "If he was sitting there, he might have noticed the seam of the door isn't quite hidden by the trim piece."

Inspector Longly put on his glove again and moved the roll of paper to the desk. After searching for a moment, he located and retrieved the penknife from the desk set that had been tipped onto the floor. Longly slit the piece of tape that held the papers together in a tube.

The roll sprang open, revealing a map of India in sepia tones. Unlike the crisp white paper on the outside, the map was faded and the edges crinkled. Longly looked through the stack of maps, which kept their curved shape. Most of the maps were faded and yellowed, and the ink on many of them was a tea-stained brown.

Longly examined the front and back of the maps as he worked his way through them. He seemed to have forgotten I was behind him, and I remained silent and still.

"At first glance, it appears we have seven maps of India signed by Rudyard Kipling, five of Europe with the signature of Charles Darwin, six Italian maps with the signature of Lord Byron, three of Scotland with Sir Walter Scott's signature, and one of Israel, but no signature on that one. That's considerably more than he showed to Sir Leo. These will have to be analyzed, of course, but it seems Mr. Payne could match a map to anyone's taste."

The sergeant scratched his hairline as he glanced around the room. "So you think someone was looking for these maps?"

Longly turned to me. He hadn't forgotten I was in the room because he didn't hesitate or look surprised when he saw me. "Are you sure Miss Miller took a sleeping draught last night?"

"You think Miss Miller might have done this? But she already had her—um—the item she wanted," I amended with a glance at the constables.

Longly motioned for the sergeant to take charge of

the maps and escorted me out to the corridor. "I have to consider all possibilities, Miss Belgrave."

"Miss Miller certainly seemed sleepy when I spoke to her. I suppose it's possible she could have been acting, but I don't think so. And I doubt she would do something like that." I gestured to the green room. "I think she might have wanted to search Mr. Payne's room, but I don't know that she'd have had the courage to do it."

"She does seem a bit timid," Longly said, "but she searched Mr. Payne's body. That took gumption. However, I doubt she'd have the knowledge to pick a lock." Longly gave me a quick smile. "It's a skill that most people don't have—thank goodness."

"The locks on the doors are not incredibly secure. If you jiggle the key from one door in any of the other locks, you can usually get the door open. That's another bit of knowledge I accumulated during my childhood with my cousins," I added quickly. I didn't want him to think I'd been creeping about the halls last night trying my key in the green room's lock. "But I don't think Miss Miller would have cared about the maps. Her only interest was in retrieving her letter, which she had last evening in her bedroom."

Longly looked back to the green room and spoke more to himself than to me. "Another option is that someone decided to take advantage of Mr. Payne's death and help themselves to the remaining maps, the three that Mr. Payne let be known he still had for sale, but they couldn't locate them."

"But no one seems to be in a perilous financial situation," I said, then mentally added, *except me*. But I wasn't going to point that fact out to Longly. Fortunately, the sergeant called him, and I left quickly, making my way to the billiard room, where I hoped to find Jasper. We needed to compare notes.

CHAPTER ELEVEN

*J*asper was indeed in the billiard room. He was slumped in a club chair with his elbow propped on the chair arm, massaging his brow.

I sat down in the chair beside him. "Good morning, Jasper."

He lifted his fingers and looked at me from under them.

"Hello, Olive. I thought you'd be along soon."

"Still recovering from last night, I see."

"Yes," he said, and I thought there was a hint of wariness in his tone. "Olive, last night—" He shifted. "It's a bit foggy, but I seem to remember being in your room . . .?"

"Yes, you were." He pressed his fingers down over his eyes for a moment as I added, "You were quite insistent about informing me about what you'd discovered at the pub."

His fingers lifted again. "And was that . . . all?"

"Well, you had some rather nice things to say about my perfume."

Relief washed over his face, and I decided not to mention that he nearly kissed me—or that I'd wanted to kiss him. Best to bury that . . . little aberration and go on as we'd been.

"Oh. Right. Good." He squinted at me as if he was trying to work out if I was holding something back, then said, "Good. Then on to sleuthing. It's been a productive morning."

"Really? What have you been doing?"

"As I said, sleuthing."

"Are you sure? You look so comfortable."

"Believe me, my head isn't comfortable at all." He slowly rearranged himself in his chair and clasped his hands across his chest. "I've been gathering information —through emissaries." He squinted at me. "You look animated. I suppose you've been incredibly busy and productive this morning."

"Several things have happened. Our childhood hiding places came in handy just now." Without going into detail about Miss Miller's letter because I'd promised to keep that bit secret, I told Jasper about Miss Miller's presence in the conservatory, her accusation that Payne was passing off forged signatures on the maps, and the discovery of the abundance of maps hidden in Payne's room.

"Maps with forged signatures," Jasper said. "Hardly something to kill someone over."

"I agree, but I can't work out any other reason someone would want to do away with Mr. Payne."

"Therein lies the problem. My sleuthing has brought the same issue to light."

"Tell me what you've learned." I burrowed deeper into the chair cushions, settling in to listen. "I'm curious about how you've done it, seeing as you're all but incapacitated."

"You forget about Grigsby. Never underestimate the power of a good gentleman's gentleman."

"I never forget about Grigsby," I said.

"You say that as if he's frightening."

"He's like an English bulldog when it comes to guarding you."

Jasper grinned. "He tends to be a bit overprotective, but we all have our little foibles." Jasper pushed himself higher in the chair. "I thought it would be a good idea to check on the servants. Since Mr. Payne had a tendency to behave so . . . badly, shall we say, I thought perhaps he might have, um, tried to force himself on one of the female servants. Perhaps Peter interceded and was injured."

"And the female servant bashed Mr. Payne on the head then fled? It seems . . . unlikely."

"And convoluted," Jasper said with a sigh. He was grasping at anything he could think of to help Peter.

I understood that, but I felt I had to point out the other flaw in the theory. I made my tone mild as I said, "Besides, Gwen knew about Mr. Payne's . . . tendencies. She'd taken steps to protect everyone—"

"But people don't always do as they're told."

"That is true," I allowed.

Jasper sighed again, deeper this time. "But you're

133

correct in your assessment of the idea. Grigsby made discreet inquiries among the servants, but it was a dead end. With the dinner party plans, it was all hands on deck, so to speak. As far as Grigsby was able to determine, no one was missing or unaccounted for any time during the evening. He also learned the police asked the same questions. From their lack of interest in the servants today, it seems as if the police have reached the same conclusion—that the staff wasn't involved in Mr. Payne's death."

"If that's the case, then the murderer could only be one of the guests."

"It appears so." Jasper leaned forward. "The murder must be something rooted in Mr. Payne's actions or his background. We need to know more about him. Inspector Longly apparently feels the same way. Grigsby learned the inspector has been asking everyone what they know about Mr. Payne's background, who his people were, where he was from, that sort of thing."

"Inspector Longly asked me those questions. I couldn't tell him anything, though. And I don't think any of the houseguests are going to be much help. I don't believe Mr. Payne was known to anyone before he arrived. He came at the invitation of Uncle Leo."

"He had to be known to someone here. People don't generally do away with new acquaintances."

"I can ask Uncle Leo how he came to invite him," I said.

"Most likely, Mr. Payne contacted Sir Leo and offered his maps for sale. It's a common practice. Once it's known that you have a penchant for collecting a certain thing, word gets out. I receive letters of that kind occasionally in reference to books." Jasper had an extensive library that ranged from antique first editions to the latest crime novels.

I thought back, trying to remember any tidbit that Payne mentioned about his personal life. "During our dinner conversation, I believe Mr. Payne made a passing mention of a flat in London," I said finally. It was all I could think of other than the detail about selling maps.

"Rather unspecific."

"Quite." I pushed myself out of the chair. "I'll track down Uncle Leo."

"And I believe I'll write a few letters to collector friends of mine. Perhaps they've some information about Mr. Payne." Jasper levered himself out of his chair more slowly than I had. He remained motionless for a moment, his eyes closed. Then he blinked them open. "No more evenings at the pub. Sleuthing is more taxing than I would've imagined."

Jasper left to write his letters, and I went to Uncle Leo's study. I tapped on the door, but no one answered. I'd hoped I might find him there, but I knew it was unlikely. Uncle Leo was usually only in his study for a few hours in the evening. He liked to be out and about on the estate during the day, and his estate steward, Mr. Davis, hadn't returned from London.

I lingered a moment when I entered the room, scrutinizing the framed maps that covered the wood-paneled walls. I'd never considered antique maps as more than an interesting hobby of Uncle Leo's. Could a piece of paper be at the root of Payne's death? It seemed unlikely. Perhaps one of the maps that had been hidden in the cupboard was incredibly valuable. But then, why kill Payne? It wasn't as if he'd been guarding the maps when he died. If the maps were the goal, it would make more sense to slip into the green room while everyone was occupied—say, during teatime—make a search, and remove the map. Payne might not have even noticed anything was missing until later because he had so many maps with him.

I decided I wasn't going to work out what had happened through mental cogitation and went to find Brimble. He had an uncanny knack of knowing every-one's location and could probably pinpoint Uncle Leo's whereabouts within a few feet. But as I rounded the newel post at the bottom of the staircase, I met Sonia, who had a dazed look on her face. Her skin had a sickly gray undertone to it as well, and her arms were drawn into her sides as if she were cold or in pain.

I normally avoided interactions with my step-mother, but I couldn't walk away from her with only a polite greeting in passing. Thinking of her prior bout with sickness that Gwen had mentioned, I asked, "Are you ill, Sonia? Do you need to sit down?"

"No, I don't. Oh, it's appalling, just appalling. They've taken Peter away in the police motor. I saw it from the drawing room windows."

My heart sank. Gwen and her parents would be so distressed. It wasn't a complete shock to me because I'd heard Longly ask Peter to accompany him to the police station this morning, but Sonia hadn't been in the room.

"That is distressing, but I imagine it's just to answer questions. He'll be back soon, I'm sure." I said the words, hoping they were true. Before Sonia could notice the lack of certainty in my tone, I added, "Let's get you some water or a cup of tea."

She blinked and seemed to come out of her mental fog, which was an unusual state for her. I was surprised at her reaction. Sonia had a stoic nature and wasn't given to either bursts of emotion or bouts of preoccupation. My father spent most of his day lost in thought about his writing. Sonia was down-to-earth and practical.

"No. I'm fine," she said, but her voice caught. She cleared her throat. "I'm only concerned for—the family. How ghastly this must be for Caroline and Leo. Think of what people will say." She glanced over my shoulder to the stairs and made a visible effort to calm herself. She drew a breath and switched on a strained smile. "Cecil, dear," she said. "I thought you would be in the library all morning."

Father waved a notebook as he trotted down the last flight of stairs. "I forgot this, and I can't get along without it. Good morning, Olive."

I was pleased to see Father moving so agilely. He'd been frail since his illness, but today he looked like his old self. He joined us on the main floor and waggled the notebook. "I knew I had some good notes in here about David's time hiding from Saul. I'll leave you ladies. Must get my thoughts down—" He took half a step away, then stopped and studied Sonia's face. "Are you all right, my dear?"

She widened her tense smile. "Yes, of course. Everything's fine—completely fine. You go on to the library. I'll come find you at lunch. I know how immersed you become in your books."

Father chuckled. "Indeed, I do. It's a good thing you're around, my dear. I might not eat until tea, otherwise."

With a pat on my shoulder, Father left for the library, his head bent as he paged through his notebook. I knew that within a few steps he was already engrossed in his notes, his thoughts with his writing, not us.

As soon as he turned away, Sonia's face transformed back into its strained lines. She made a move to leave as well, but I put a hand on her arm. If Father had noticed Sonia's distress, something was definitely amiss. The answer flashed through my mind. "You know something, something about Peter—no, about *Mr. Payne.* You became sick and had to leave shortly after the guests arrived. You're never ill. And you're not simply worried about the family's reputation. It's more than that."

Sonia had flinched when I said Payne's name. "Shh!" Father had disappeared into the library as I spoke, and now she glanced around the entry hall, the hiss echoing up to the ceiling mural. "Someone might hear."

"I rather doubt it." I looked up the deserted staircase. "We're alone." The black-and-white marble floor of the entry hall was as blank as a chessboard after the pieces had been swept away at the end of a game. "Clearly, you know something about Mr. Payne—that's what's eating away at you, making you ill. Whatever it is, you must tell Longly—"

"No!" Her sharp word reverberated off the marble. She breathed in through her nose, then said in a normal tone, "Anyone could come down the stairs or be lurking in one of the rooms. I must go—"

She made a move toward the stairs. I stepped into her path and crossed my arms. "What do you know?" If she knew something that might help Peter, I wasn't about to let her leave without finding out what it was.

The natural downturn of her lips deepened as she studied me, then she let out a short huff of breath. "All right. I will tell you, but only because I realize you won't be put off. And you can . . . help." She said the last word as if she'd eaten a bite of food that had gone off. "Come out to the garden. It should be safe to talk there."

Usually I'd be less than interested in strolling outdoors on a frigid morning—especially with Sonia—and would find some excuse to avoid it, but today I didn't hesitate.

A few minutes later I was wrapping my scarf around my neck and buttoning my coat as I followed Sonia across the terrace. We descended the flight of steps to the gardens. Her skin looked even worse in the wintry sunlight, and she pressed a hand to her midriff as if she had a stomach ache.

The gardens were bare of flowers, and the beds had been banked with mulch. The flower beds, a pattern of brown squares, circles, and triangles, stretched out to the line of greenhouses in the distance. We turned down the path that led to the Neptune and mermaid fountain at the center of the gardens. At our backs, the windows of Parkview sparkled in the sunlight. The only sounds were the plink of water as the ice that had coated the fountains and benches melted in the sun, and the crunch of our shoes against the sandy path. The fountain's swirling mass of movement frozen in marble rose several feet above our heads.

In the summer, the central fountain with its gentle burble was one of my favorite places, but the harsh winter light picked out the pockmarks in the statues and the traces of mold in the crevices. When we were children we'd toss coins and bits of gravel in the fountain, aiming for Neptune's trident. Now instead of pennies sparkling under the water, there was only a smattering of dead leaves caught in a thin layer of ice that filled the basin.

"This should be private enough." My breath came out in little white vapor clouds.

Sonia gripped the basin's edge. "I can't believe this has happened." A spark of her usual forceful personality showed for a moment, which I found strangely comforting. With her gaze focused on the carved edge of the fountain rim, she said, "You're right. I do know something about Mr. Payne. I recognized him straightaway that first moment in the drawing room. He was my husband."

CHAPTER TWELVE

"*M*r. Payne was your husband? You mean —you're *divorced?*"

My mind spun with questions. Did Father know? He couldn't. He'd never marry a divorcée. Even though he'd retired from serving as a vicar, I knew there were certain standards he felt an obligation to uphold.

Sonia jumped as if someone had dropped an icicle down her collar. "No." Her gaze skittered around the garden. "I'm not divorced." She'd lowered her voice to a whisper on the word *divorced* as if the word itself was abhorrent.

"Then I don't understand."

She threw me an irritated glance as she pushed away from the fountain and strode a few steps. I thought she was about to stalk off and leave me there, but she stopped by a stone bench. "I knew it was Simon the moment he walked into the drawing room."

"Simon?" Perhaps she was sick—not physically ill,

but maybe something was a little off . . . mentally. "Why don't we sit down on this bench for a moment?" I'd always found her irritating, but I'd never doubted her sanity.

She flicked her fingers in an impatient gesture. "I'm not confused. The man who died in the conservatory wasn't Vincent Payne. He was Simon Adams. Simon was impersonating Vincent." She blew out another breath as if she had just completed a long hike up a difficult trail. "It's a complicated story."

She seemed to be in her right mind. She was speaking evenly, not ranting or over-excited. I did want to hear what Sonia thought had happened, so I said, "I'm in no rush to get back to the house."

"I suppose I'd better start at the beginning—years ago when the three of us were children living in the same village," Sonia continued in her flat tone. "Vincent Payne, Simon Adams, and I grew up in Clifton Green."

I shook my head. "I haven't heard of it."

"It's a tiny village in Surrey. Vincent Payne—the real Vincent Payne—lived with his uncle, who was the largest landowner for miles around. Simon's father was the greengrocer. My father was a doctor. Vincent was quite shy and reserved. Simon was always joking and laughing, and he could make the silliest faces." Her expression softened. "When we grew up, Simon and I, we . . . well, we thought we were in love and wanted to marry."

Sonia tested the marble bench for dampness, then eased herself down onto it. "My father forbade Simon and me to marry, of course. He would have accepted Vincent Payne as a son-in-law, but not the greengrocer's son."

My mind reeled as I sat on the next bench over, barely noticing the chilliness of the stone. It was difficult to imagine Sonia in a Romeo and Juliet situation—much less as a rebellious young woman.

"We married," Sonia said, her voice flat. "We were old enough. We moved to London, and Simon found a job working for a greengrocer." She stared at the empty flowerbeds for a moment. "Unfortunately, my father was right. We weren't suited. It became apparent after a few years. We fought constantly. When we were young, I liked his teasing. He used to say he was the only person who could make me smile—and he could. I was a rather serious child." She gave me a sideways look. The natural downward curve at the corners of her mouth vanished for a moment as a small smile crossed her face.

Was she making a joke? For a moment I was tempted to reply, "No!" in a scoffing tone, but I refrained. I didn't want to break the fragile atmosphere and bring her story to a halt. I settled for, "Indeed."

"Indeed, I was," Sonia said. "Simon had a sense of play and fun that I didn't. I liked that." She sighed as the tiny smile disappeared. "It was only after we were married that I began to see sides of his personality that I'd ignored. His teasing could have a vicious edge to it, but if that had been all, I could have endured it. But then I learned he hadn't been faithful. He was too selfish, too short-sighted." She shook her head and looked away. "Too driven by his own desires."

I thought of Gwen's description of Payne's pushy insistence she go for a walk with him and of his behavior toward Gigi in the woods. The Mr. Payne I'd met certainly acted like the man Sonia was describing.

"Eventually, I told him I wished we'd never married." She gripped the edge of the stone bench with both hands and dipped her head. "It was awful. But the war came, and Simon went off to fight. I'd trained as a nurse and worked for a year before Simon and I married, so I applied for a job in a hospital. Nurses were in demand, and it didn't take long for me to find work." Sonia brushed a trace of dirt off the bench. "A few months later I received a telegram. He'd been killed."

"I'm sorry." My heart squeezed in sympathy. I'd known that flare of fear as the telegram boy approached.

We sat in silence for a few moments. Eventually, I said, "So when you met Mr. Payne a few days ago, you thought he was Simon? Are you sure it was him?" I asked as gently as I could. So many families of men who had been declared missing in action or who had died and been buried on the battlefield grasped at any shred of hope that their loved ones were actually still alive. Without a body to bury and a grave to visit, many people found it difficult to believe their sons or fathers were really dead. They wanted to believe a mistake had been made. The false hope of the war veterans' families was a fertile ground for conmen and shysters—and that seemed to fit right in with Payne's apparently fraud-prone personality.

Sonia raised her head and let out a sharp laugh. "Oh, it was Simon, all right. I knew him immediately. The way he moved, the way he spoke—" My expression must have held a hint of skepticism because she added, "Simon had a small dimple in the center of his chin and a chicken pox scar just at the tail end of his left eyebrow. It was him. Even though he was going by the name Vincent Payne, he was Simon Adams." Her voice turned bitter. "And when he recognized me and realized I'd married a vicar, he thought it was a great joke, a woman who was still actually married had committed bigamy—and with a retired vicar. He found it extremely entertaining."

"Did no one else realize you recognized him?"

"I didn't stay long enough for anyone to notice. I was so shocked and distraught, I had to get out of that room, out of Parkview. I told your father I had a horrible ache in my head, and we left straightaway. And all the while, Simon—or Mr. Payne, as he was calling himself—had that smirk on his face. He knew my secret and couldn't wait to taunt me about it."

"But wasn't he afraid of you? You could call his bluff and reveal he wasn't Mr. Payne."

"I had so much more to lose than he did, though. And he knew it."

I shifted on the bench and tucked my scarf closer around my neck. This information was a lot to take in, and I wasn't sure I believed Sonia. She was so adamant the man wasn't Payne, but she was adamant about everything—what was best for Father . . . and me, for that matter. She'd never second-guess herself, so I asked about Payne instead. "Do you know what happened? How this, um, Simon Adams came to be known as Mr. Payne, who was his childhood acquaintance?"

"With Simon it was always better to confront him, so we returned to Parkview the next afternoon. I sent Simon a message, and he agreed to meet me in the courtyard."

So, when I'd seen her from the window, the man in the shadows had been Payne—I couldn't think of him as Simon, no matter what Sonia said.

"I demanded to know what he was doing impersonating Vincent. He said, 'Impersonate? I *am* Vincent Payne. The British Army says so.'" She gave a little shake of her head in what I thought was irritation, then added, "He and Vincent served together. According to Simon, there was an attack, and a shell went off near him and Vincent. When Simon awoke in the casualty clearing station, the nurses and doctors called him by Vincent's name. Simon told me he was in terrible pain and didn't remember much more than that. He said he wasn't sure what happened, but he thinks Vincent's identity tag was found beside him, and the stretcher-bearer must have assumed it belonged to him—at least that was Simon's story."

"You don't believe it?" I asked.

"I believe parts of it," she said, picking her words. "The identity discs were terribly flimsy and easily destroyed. The identities of many—um—corpses—were completely lost because the identity discs didn't stay intact with the bodies. Misidentification was quite common. I even saw it happen a few times at the hospital." She stood, buried her hands into her coat pockets, and paced between the bench and the fountain. "So, yes, it's possible Simon's story is true, but I did wonder if he . . . helped . . . create the situation."

"Wouldn't someone from his platoon have recognized he wasn't Mr. Payne?"

"Only two other people from his platoon survived. After the casualty clearing station, Simon would have been sent on to England. He was probably with strangers the entire time." She shrugged with her hands still tucked in her pockets. "Whatever happened—whether Simon instigated the misidentification, or it was truly a mistake—he was accepted as Vincent Payne."

"Which sounds as if it would be a, um, social step up?" Having been in a strained financial situation myself, I could understand the temptation of assuming the identity of someone better off than oneself.

"From the son of a greengrocer to the landed gentry?" Sonia said. "It was a giant stride up the social ladder."

"But what about the uncle and the rest of his family? Surely they would have recognized Simon was an imposter. And Simon's parents? What about them?" Had he let them think he was dead?

"Vincent's uncle had passed away a few years before the war, leaving Vincent an extremely wealthy man. Simon's parents contracted pneumonia and died before the war began. Simon didn't have any other family." She paused a moment, then went on, "Vincent's only close relative, an aunt, lives in South Africa with her husband, so there was no immediate family to contradict Simon when he became Vincent. I never returned to Clifton Green. My father cut me off when I married Simon. Even if he hadn't done that, Father retired to a little seaside cottage in Hastings after the war, so I had no reason to return to the village either."

"But surely Mr. Payne, or Simon, as you knew him, would run across *someone* who had known them both and be recognized—"

Sonia shook her head. "Vincent and Simon resembled each other. They both had brown hair and brown eyes and were of a similar height. Old Mrs. Oglethorpe used to say that Vincent and Simon could have been mistaken for cousins."

She paced faster, the fabric of her coat stretching tight over her shoulders as she pushed her hands deeper into her pockets. "Vincent's money was a tidy little sum, which I'm sure was part of the reason Simon did it. Impersonating Vincent also solved the problem of the estrangement between us. I didn't want to be married any longer and neither did he. So he became Vincent Payne."

"And he let you think he was dead . . . and marry another man."

"Yes." Anger and worry infused the single word. "I'm sure he never even thought of the possibility I'd marry again. Simon was short-sighted. He never thought beyond the next day or week." She stopped pacing and rubbed her hand across her eyes for a moment, then came and sat on the bench beside me. "You can see why you must find out who killed Simon —or Vincent Payne, as I suppose we should continue to call him now. He'd become Vincent. Your father *cannot* know. He'd—" Her voice cracked, and she put a hand to her mouth for a moment. She pulled herself together and continued in a measured tone. "Your father is a wonderful man. So kind and gentle, and I never intended to deceive him. I thought Simon was dead. Truly, I did."

"You didn't tell him you'd married before the war and were a widow?"

"No. I wanted to forget Simon and the war and all that. It's difficult for me to speak about the war. I only told your father in general terms what I did during that time. It's too painful to speak of the specifics. I don't let myself dwell on what I saw. I can't. And I was"—she drew in a breath before she continued—"ashamed of marrying Simon. He wasn't an honorable man like your father. I thought that if your father knew about him, he might not want to marry me. You can see, can't you, that your father can't know about Simon? Not now. Not after I didn't tell him. He *mustn't* find out."

"Oh my." It was all I could say. Father was the sweetest man, but there were a few things he wouldn't tolerate—lying being at the top of the list. The only time Father had paddled me and sent me to my room without supper was when I was five and I'd lied to him, saying I'd spent the afternoon in the garden. In reality, I'd slipped away to visit my cousins at Parkview.

"Please help me, Olive. You've handled sensitive things like this before." Sonia seemed to be so worried about Father discovering she'd been married to Payne that she'd completely overlooked the fact that she had an excellent motive for his murder. I hesitated, and she said, "Oh! You think *I* could have killed him." Her surprise seemed genuine.

"Did you?" I asked. "It would solve one of your problems."

"But create so many more." Her voice was filled with conviction. "No, I didn't kill him. Believe me, there were days when I wanted to" —she drew herself up —"but I'm a nurse. I don't harm people. I help them heal and recover."

"You were in a precarious situation with Mr. Payne when he was alive. He could have blackmailed you."

"He wasn't interested in money. He had much more than your father and I. No, he didn't want money. He simply wanted to . . . take pleasure in my discomfort."

"You think Mr. Payne would have gone away at the end of the party and left you alone?"

"I know he would have. He even said to me, 'Don't worry, Sonia, I won't make trouble for you. I'll go quietly, but I'll enjoy watching you squirm until I leave.'"

"What a dreadful man."

"Yes, he was. But I assure you I didn't kill him. Will you help me?"

I wasn't sure if I believed her. There were so many layers of deception—Sonia's and Payne's—and she was asking me to keep something from Father, to lie by omission. But she'd nursed Father back to health. His improved condition was thanks to her. For that alone, I owed her a debt. "I'll do what I can—"

She gripped my hand. "Oh, thank you, Olive. I know you'll sort it out."

CHAPTER THIRTEEN

*W*hen Sonia and I parted, I went to my room and dug through my handbag, looking for a calling card. I knew I'd tucked it away in case I needed it later. I was torn, not sure if I believed Sonia's story. But why would she make it up? Clearly, she was distraught and worried, a state I'd never seen her in. The first thing to do was to verify her story, if possible. If what she said was true, it added a new complexity to Payne's death. If I took Sonia at her word and believed she hadn't killed Payne to protect herself, it raised more questions.

I found the card in my handbag underneath the metal makeup compact in the shape of a small hand-gun. Jasper had given me the compact to use as a deterrent in case I was ever in a situation where I needed something that looked as if I had a weapon. It had certainly come in handy on one occasion, and I always carried it in my handbag now.

I took the calling card and went down to Uncle Leo's study to use the telephone on Mr. Davis's desk because it was more private than the entry hall, where the other telephone was installed. Uncle Leo didn't like speaking on the telephone and preferred to have Mr. Davis use "the instrument," as Uncle Leo called it. I settled into Mr. Davis's chair at his cluttered desk, which was tucked away in a little alcove in the study. As I drew the telephone toward me, I noticed an envelope with Uncle Leo's untidy scrawl, *Invoice for maps—Payne,* which reminded me I still needed to track down Uncle Leo and ask about the maps.

I pushed the stack with the envelope on top of it to the side. After receiving the maps from Payne, Uncle Leo must have dropped the invoice off for Mr. Davis to file. I wondered what would happen with the maps. I was sure Longly would have the signatures on all the maps, including Uncle Leo's, checked. Would Uncle Leo's maps be returned after the investigation? Would he want them back if the signatures were forgeries?

I lifted the handset and asked to be connected to the number written on the card. When the call was put through, a gravelly voice answered.

I asked, "May I speak to Mr. Frederick Boggs, please?"

"I'll see if he's around," the man said, then raised his voice without bothering to move the telephone as he shouted, "Boggs! Telephone for you. Someone posh, by the sound of it."

When Boggs came on the line, I said, "Hello, Mr. Boggs. This is Olive Belgrave."

"Miss Belgrave, hello." His accent had lost a little of its starchiness now that he wasn't working in an opulent London townhouse.

"How are you, Mr. Boggs?"

"Fine. Just fine. Things are a bit slow, but better than my last situation."

"I'm glad to hear you're well. I have a small task that I can't complete myself. Would you be interested in taking it on? I'd pay you, of course. It would involve traveling to a village in Surrey and asking some questions."

"Yes, I'm interested. Very interested."

"Wonderful." I told him the specifics, and we agreed on an amount for the job. "Send a telegram to Parkview Hall, Derbyshire, with the details on what you learn, please."

"I'll go there this afternoon and see what I can find out," Boggs said before we rang off.

When I came out of the study, it was close to lunch, so I went along to the dining room, where a cold buffet had been laid out. Miss Miller and Aunt Caroline were seated at the table, deep in a discussion of their bridge game. I greeted them and took a sandwich from one of the trays. I chatted with Miss Miller and Aunt Caroline as I ate, but I didn't have much of an appetite. I had too much on my mind.

I left the dining room and found Jasper in the entry hall, slipping his spectacles into a pocket as he handed off several letters to a footman. "See these are put in the post today," he said to the footman, then caught sight of me. Apparently, he'd shaken off the last effects of his night at the pub. He was moving at a faster pace now and didn't squint against the light as he came across to me. "Olive, where did you disappear off to?"

"The gardens. I have something to tell you . . . in a moment," I said as Gigi drifted down the stairs, making her first appearance of the day.

She wore a cardigan, white blouse, and knit skirt, which would have been a tame outfit, but with her lithe movements and the sway of her hips as she descended, she looked anything but demure. "Good morning," she said as she joined us. "I suppose both of you have already been up for hours and breakfasted with the sunrise."

"Seeing as it's November, that's not a great challenge to achieve," Jasper said, his tone teasing.

"Well, that's fine for you," Gigi said. "I make it a firm policy to never have breakfast before noon." She turned to me. "I'm so glad your Aunt Caroline isn't one of those hostesses who has everything cleared away by ten o'clock."

"Well, breakfast has been cleared, but there's a cold buffet laid out in the dining room. I'm sure you can find something to nibble. And Brimble saved a selection of newspapers for you to choose from for your crossword." I'd seen them stacked on the sideboard this morning.

Gigi brightened. "Brilliant." She left, moving in a more energetic way than she had before.

Jasper turned to me. "Crosswords?"

"She's a wizard at them. Does them in ink. In school,

we used to challenge her to see if she could complete the difficult ones in half an hour. She always managed it."

"I'd never have thought it of her."

"I know. She seems empty-headed, but she's quite clever. Of course, she doesn't want anyone to know that. But I was at school with her and know her secret. She only put a little effort into her studies and always made high marks. But enough about Gigi. I have news. We must go somewhere we won't be overheard." Now I understood Sonia's caution about speaking in the echoey entry hall. The click of billiard balls indicated that the room was occupied, probably by Captain Ingle-brook, and Father was using the library. If we went to any of the main rooms, we might be interrupted. "I know, let's go up to the small sitting room."

"Good idea." Jasper motioned for me to precede him up the stairs.

"Did you hear Inspector Longly took Peter to the police station?" I asked in a low voice as we trotted upstairs.

Jasper paused on the landing, his hand gripping the newel post. "No, I didn't."

"Sonia was extremely upset. I told her I was sure it was routine, but truthfully, I'm not sure at all."

"I hope you're right about it being routine," he said and increased his pace as we climbed the rest of the stairs to the small sitting room.

Situated at the back of the house, the room was too cramped for a proper sitting room. It had been a retreat for Peter and Gwen after they left the nursery, a place they could escape Violet, who was at a pesky stage. Since Parkview was practically my second home, I was usually in the small sitting room with them, and when Jasper visited Peter during their school holidays, he'd joined us there.

I was happy to see the familiar mishmash of furniture castoffs from the rest of the house. Stacks of board games, jigsaw puzzles, and books that we'd used to pass the time during rainy days still filled the shelves. The only "new" thing was a weathered roll-top desk Gwen had installed at one side of the room where she handled much of the running of the household.

I settled into the squishy chair covered in faded chintz, and Jasper took his usual place on the window seat, his back propped up against the wall and his long legs stretched out across the seat.

"I had a chat with Sonia this morning." I told him everything Sonia had said about Payne. Sonia hadn't been pleased when I'd informed her I'd have to share her story with Jasper, but I'd convinced her Jasper was trustworthy. I needed to be able to share the details with him. Because of his weak eyesight, Jasper had spent the war working at a desk in the war office, which meant he had the contacts to check the story that Payne had told Sonia—at least, I hoped he knew the right people to ask to confirm or discount the story.

Jasper's eyebrows soared when I told him of Sonia's insistence that Payne was actually Simon Adams, but he listened without interrupting me until I'd recounted everything. "What do you think of Mr. Payne's story?" I asked.

Jasper squinted as he looked out the window to the gardens. "It's not impossible that the identity discs were switched." He spoke slowly, choosing his words. "And the fact that most of the platoon didn't survive—well, that was all too common as well. It would make it much easier for him to continue living as Vincent Payne. It sounds as if there were few people who would question his identity. But it puts your stepmother in a sticky situation."

"Quite. She swears she didn't harm him, and"—I shook my head—"I'm astounded I'm saying this, but I'm leaning toward believing her. Could you verify what Mr. Payne told her?"

"I'll certainly do my best. It will be difficult to do it today as it's Saturday, but I'll try. I have a friend . . ." He swung his feet off the bench, then noticed the time on the carriage clock. "No, it's one o'clock. He'll be at lunch. I'll have to contact him later." Jasper settled himself on the bench again. "The part about Sonia's childhood in the village, now that's another story."

"I have Boggs working on that."

Jasper said, "Hiring employees now, are you?"

"Only for an occasional odd job. Boggs seemed like a good person to keep in touch with."

"Yes, he's . . . resourceful."

I shifted, curling my legs up and settling deeper into the chair. "So, until we hear back from Boggs or you can make your inquiries, what can we do here? The problem we have is the suspect pool is so small. I'm afraid Longly—or his superintendent—will focus only on Peter and Miss Miller. And perhaps Deena," I added. "We mustn't forget about her."

"You think Deena murdered Mr. Payne?"

"She found the body, which makes her the main suspect by default—at least it always does in the crime fiction books you've lent me."

"But what was her motive?"

We both sat in silence as the carriage clock ticked.

Finally, I said, "Perhaps Mr. Payne tried to take advantage of her as he did with Gigi. She struck him and then dragged him to the fountain to make it look like an accident?" Just speaking the idea aloud made me want to discard it. It was too flimsy.

"It's possible," Jasper said, "but if that's the case, why wouldn't she have told Longly or someone else what happened? There was no need to make it look like an accident. In fact, it would be better for her if she didn't do that."

"Fear that the police wouldn't think it was self-defense?" I asked, testing out the idea, then I shook my head. "But that doesn't fit. If Dr. Grimshaw is right and someone used a spade to hit Mr. Payne, where would Deena get it? Ross always puts his garden tools away in the cupboards at the back of the conservatory. If Mr. Payne attacked Deena near the fountain, I doubt she ran to the cupboards to look for something to defend herself. How would she even know the spades were kept there? No, it would make much more sense for her to simply run out of the conservatory. It's a shorter distance to either door than it is to the cupboard."

"Miss Miller was also in the conservatory, don't forget."

"She's frail, though. Could she drag Mr. Payne across the floor, not to mention hit him on the head? Miss Miller is small like me. She'd have to have stood on a chair to bean Mr. Payne near the top of his head."

"And I doubt Mr. Payne would have stood quietly in place while she clambered up on a chair with a spade in her hand," Jasper said. "But she did want the mysterious envelope. I think you're holding out on me. There's got to be more to that story."

"As I told you earlier today, I've been sworn to secrecy, but I assure you the contents of the envelope are irrelevant to our inquiry. You're correct. Miss Miller did want the letter, but I don't think she'd attack him for it. I'm sure she'd ask someone else—another man, my Father or even Uncle Leo—for help in convincing Mr. Payne to give back her letter before she'd resort to violence."

"What about Gigi?" Jasper asked. "If she's able to whip through crosswords as quickly as you say, she's cleverer than I realized."

"You mean she was getting back at Mr. Payne for him taking advantage in the woods?" I considered the idea, then said, "No. I don't think it was Gigi. The way the murderer tried to make it look as if Mr. Payne had fallen and hit his head—no, that's too meticulous for Gigi. I can imagine her doing something in a moment of passion—say, shooting someone—but dragging a body around to create a certain scene? Not Gigi."

"I'm making a mental note to never anger her," Jasper said with a trace of humor, but then he added, his tone serious, "Are you absolutely sure, old bean? Crosswords are tedious. One must have patience to complete them."

"I agree. Despite that, I still don't think Gigi did it."

"Then who's left?" Jasper asked.

"Captain Inglebrook?" I replied, doubt heavy in my tone. "He's tall enough and strong enough to move the body."

"But again, no motive."

"That we know of," I said. "Clearly, we don't know enough about everyone here at Parkview."

The door opened and Gwen came in. "There you are. Now that I have the dinner menu settled, I've been looking all over for the two of you. Even in the midst of a crisis, household duties must be seen to." Gwen perched on the end of the worn Chesterfield sofa. "Inspector Longly took Peter to the police station, did you know?"

"Yes, I heard," I said.

"I'd thought you were going to distract him."

"I did try—"

"And the servants said the news about Mr. Payne's death is all over the village," Gwen went on, speaking over my words. "Dr. Grimshaw gossips like an old woman. He made it clear at the pub last night that he thinks Mr. Payne's death wasn't an accident, but murder." She crossed her arms. "Olive, surely you've found out *something* by now that will help Peter."

I squirmed in my chair. I'd promised Miss Miller I wouldn't divulge her secret about her brother being duped with the forged signatures or the fact that Payne had blackmailed her with a stolen love letter. And I'd promised Sonia I'd keep her secrets about Payne. That was entirely too many secrets. Nevertheless, I'd keep my word. "I'm making progress," I said.

Gwen's eyebrows came together as she frowned. "That's all? You're making progress?"

Jasper leaned forward, drawing Gwen's attention away from me. "What we need is more information about Mr. Payne." I shot him a warning look, but he went on smoothly, "About what Mr. Payne did once he arrived here at Parkview. How he spent his time."

"Yes," I said. "The only thing we can say with any certainty is that he sold Uncle Leo maps with dubious signatures."

Gwen said, "Which Inspector Longly has taken away."

It was another black mark against Inspector Longly in Gwen's mind. "That's part of his job," I said. "Those maps are evidence." Gwen sent me a look that said she didn't agree, but before she could launch into a speech, I went on, "There had to be some sort of incident or encounter that was the catalyst for the murderer." I just hoped it wasn't Sonia's meeting her not-dead husband who was masquerading as a childhood friend. The scandal that would stir up, not to mention the hurt that would cause Father—I shifted my mind away from that track. I'd wait and see what Boggs turned up before I resorted to those sorts of thoughts.

Gwen said, "Mr. Payne didn't know anyone here at Parkview. So, yes, something must have happened . . ."

I exchanged a glance with Jasper to warn him to keep quiet about whom Mr. Payne might or might not have known before he arrived. Gwen pushed off from the Chesterfield and went to her desk, where she picked up paper and a pencil. "I'll figure out Mr. Payne's movements. Brimble will know where the guests were."

A deep voice sounded from the door. "Having a council of war?"

We all swiveled around.

Peter stood in the doorway. Gwen dropped her paper and pencil and rushed across the room to embrace him. "You're back."

"At least for the moment."

Gwen pulled back from him, hands still on his arms as she looked into his face. "Was it horribly grim?"

"On the contrary, they were extremely polite. Polite, but relentless." His bruised eye still looked terrible, but it was the way he moved into the room and dropped onto the sofa that worried me. He let his head fall back against the cushions and closed his eyes.

Gwen pressed her lips together. The possibility of Longly patching things up with Gwen was growing smaller by the minute.

Peter opened his eyes and rolled his head to the side to make eye contact with Jasper. "I don't think they were satisfied, though."

Before Jasper could reply, Gwen asked, "Why ever not?"

"Because I couldn't answer their questions fully. I still don't remember what happened in the conservatory."

I turned in my chair. "What do you recall?"

"Not nearly enough." Peter sighed and sat up, his movements slow and laborious, reminding me of an old man. "I'd hoped my memory would be clearer today, but it's not. I know I stopped at the mirror outside the doorway to the conservatory to adjust my waistcoat, but after that"—he lifted a shoulder—"it's all blank until you arrived, Olive."

"Inspector Longly doesn't believe you?" Gwen asked, her face thunderous.

"Inspector Longly is a man who deals in facts, which I can't give him at the moment." His gaze drifted to the view of the rolling hills beyond the formal gardens. He braced his hands on his knees and stood. "I'm on my way out for a stroll. That always helps clear my head."

"Oh, don't leave now," Gwen said. "You look exhausted."

"It's how I've dealt with everything else, old girl. I can't stop now. It's all I know to do." He touched Gwen's arm, gave Jasper and me a nod, and left, his tread slow.

After Peter closed the door softly behind him, Gwen whirled around and picked up the paper and pencil. "He never would listen to reason. Why are all men so stubborn?"

I knew Gwen's irritation was a combination of

worry for Peter and anger at Longly. Jasper must have realized it too, because he didn't jump to defend his gender. He pointed to the paper. "What are you scribbling?"

"I'm making a list of what we need to do. Peter may go walk the hills, but we must make an effort to help him. I'll trace Mr. Payne's movements from the time he arrived until he went to the conservatory Friday night."

"If you see Uncle Leo, ask him how he came to invite Mr. Payne to Parkview," I said. I still hadn't seen him.

"Right." Gwen made a note, then looked up, her gaze flicking from Jasper to me. "What can you two do?"

"Jasper has a few telephone calls to make about Mr. Payne," I said.

"You can use the one in Father's study. He won't mind," Gwen said, her tone businesslike. "And you, Olive?"

"I believe I'll have a look around the conservatory now that the police have finished there."

"Whatever for?" Gwen asked. "Surely you don't think they overlooked something?"

"No, but it's dim in there in the evening, and I want to see it in the daylight. Memories can be deceptive," I said. "I also want to speak to Ross."

Gwen checked the time. "He'll probably be there now since the police had it closed off this morning. I'm sure he'll be grumbling about the constables trampling his plants." Gwen's voice indicated she thought it was a useless errand, but she didn't try to persuade me to do something else.

Our impromptu meeting broke up, and we were on our way downstairs when we met Aunt Caroline hurrying up to us, a relieved look on her face. "Oh, there you are, Gwen. Did you see Peter? He's returned."

"Yes, we spoke to him a little while ago."

"Good." Worry traced across her features. "He looked just like he did when he was seven and came down with pneumonia—all sickly and worn out. We must do something to get his mind off everything. He enjoys being out-of-doors, so a picnic at the ruin will be perfect—and something to entertain everyone else, of course. Gwen, dear, you'll speak to Cook, won't you? And have her prepare several picnic baskets for tea."

"A picnic? In this cold?" Gwen asked.

"It's pleasant outside in the sun," Aunt Caroline said. "We'll take the motors to Cormont Hill and have tea there. Don't look disapproving, Gwen. It's all decided. Miss Miller and I have already planned it and invited everyone. When one has guests, one must entertain them, murder or no murder."

Gwen said, "But a few moments ago, Peter said he was going out for a walk. He's probably already gone."

That news gave Aunt Caroline pause, then she said briskly, "Well, when he returns, Brimble can tell him where we are. Peter can meet us at the ruin."

Gwen shot me a look, which I interpreted to mean, *Mother's determined, so we might as well go along with it.*

Once Aunt Caroline got a project underway, she was relentless about its completion.

Jasper extended his arm to Aunt Caroline. "I, for one, look forward to seeing the ruin of Cormont Castle again. It's been years since I've been up there."

"They are delightful." Aunt Caroline took his arm, and they descended the stairs, leaving Gwen and me to follow. "An outing is just what we need. It will take our minds off everything and be a very pleasant afternoon, I'm sure."

CHAPTER FOURTEEN

*T*he clear bright sunlight streamed in through the glass panels of the conservatory, making it muggy and creating a dazzling effect that had me narrowing my eyes until I reached the patch of shade cast by the palms. The warmth intensified the earthy smell that permeated the air as well as the floral scents.

I wound along the path toward the sound of trickling water and the fountain. The tiles around it had been cleaned, and the iron furniture was back in place.

I followed the sound of a deep-voiced mutter to the cupboards at the back of the room, where Ross was rearranging the gardening tools. The knees of his baggy trousers were black with dirt. His flat cap was stuffed in one pocket, and garden gloves along with pruning shears caused the other side of his jacket to sag. ". . . can't expect a man to do his job without proper equipment."

"I'm sure you'll find a way," I said.

Ross looked up, and his vexed expression vanished

as he smiled, deepening the wrinkles in his tanned face. "Miss Olive, hello."

"It's good to see you, Ross."

"Thank you, miss. I know the family is always glad when you return home. Any chance of you staying on? London is a dangerous place."

"No, I'm afraid not. And it seems conservatories can be treacherous as well," I said with a significant glance over my shoulder toward the fountain.

Ross's smile disappeared. "He was a bad one."

"Mr. Payne?" Had knowledge of Payne's reputation extended to the outdoor staff?

Ross hesitated. "I don't like to talk out of turn, but he made a nuisance of himself toward the women. I saw him behave improperly toward Lady Gina out in the woods. I was about to intervene, but she took care of it."

"Yes, Gigi is quite good at taking care of herself. Did you see him behave in that manner toward anyone else?"

"No, but once is all it takes to know what sort of man he was."

"I agree with you there. I don't suppose you saw him in the conservatory the evening he died?"

"No, miss. I worked here in the morning. I was repairing a broken window in one of the greenhouses that evening."

I glanced over his shoulder at the empty spaces in the cupboard. "It looks as if the police didn't leave you much to work with."

"No, indeed. I'll have to bring over some tools from the greenhouse."

"And I'm sure you put your gardening tools away when you finished Friday?"

One corner of Ross's mouth quirked up. "You sound like that inspector chap." He leaned toward me. "I'll tell you exactly what I told him. I always clean my garden tools and then store them here. They have to be wiped down and dried or else they get rusty. That day, I transplanted some of the philodendron. They were getting too much direct sunlight. Then I worked over by the tall palm, cutting back some of the fronds. When I finished, I swept the tiles around the fountain, cleaned my tools, and then put them away."

"And your tools were in this cupboard here?" I pointed behind him. "The spades too?" There wasn't a single spade in the cabinet.

"This is where they were kept, but the police took every last one of them. I suppose I won't see any of them again, particularly if one of them was used to knock Mr. Payne on the head." Ross closed the door.

"It doesn't look as if the cupboard locks." The latch was the simple metal kind, and I didn't see any padlock lying about.

"No. There's never been a need to lock it."

"So someone could have taken a spade, but they'd need to walk back here and find it," I said.

"Yes, miss. And carry it all the way to the fountain." He shook his head. "There wasn't anything accidental about that man's death. And I don't care what the folks in the village say, Mr. Peter would never do that—whether he was in his right mind or not." Ross pinned his faded hazel gaze on me. "I hear you're good at figuring out what happened when people die, unexpected-like. I sure hope you're helping Mr. Peter clear his name."

"I'm doing everything I can." I glanced back toward the fountain. "You didn't find anything unusual here in the conservatory, something the police missed?"

He shook his head. "No, and if I found anything that could help Mr. Peter, I would have taken it to that inspector right away."

"Of course. I believe I'll wander around a bit."

Ross left, and I walked back to the center of the conservatory and stood beside the fountain, trying to work out what might have happened. I wished I had the same assurance that Jasper and Ross had about Peter's innocence. But they hadn't seen Peter's vacant gaze. I shook off that memory. It wouldn't help Peter to assume he'd murdered Payne. I had to approach the scene from a different perspective. If Peter were simply at the wrong place at the wrong time, then what had really happened here?

The overturned pot had been near the point where the path from the west wing opened into the central fountain area. Had the person who attacked Payne stood behind the rubber tree and struck as soon as Payne left the path? Perhaps the overturned iron chaise lounge had been positioned so that Payne would trip? Then, in the moment he was off-balance, the murderer brought the spade down on his head?

The iron feet on the chaise lounge screeched as I

dragged it across the tiles. I turned it on its side so that it was in the same position it had been that evening. Then I stepped over it and walked up the path a few paces, turned, and headed for the fountain.

No, there was no way someone could miss seeing the chaise lounge blocking the path, unless the person had been doing something that kept their attention off the path ahead . . . like reading. I couldn't see Payne so immersed in a book that he wasn't watching where he was going. With Father, yes, that situation would be absolutely believable, and possibly with Peter too. A little spark of excitement fired through me as I latched onto the thought.

It was true Peter wasn't as bookish as Father, but Peter had been reading the prior evening when I found him in the conservatory. And on the night Payne was killed, Peter's book about beekeeping had been lying on the floor not far from the chaise lounge. What if Peter had tripped over the chaise lounge because he was reading, and he'd hit his head and blacked out? I stood over the chaise, imagining what would happen if someone stumbled into it. The way the chair had been arranged, Peter could have hit his head on the armrest, which stuck out several inches—that could explain his black eye. The thought of plowing into the sturdy piece of metal face-first made me cringe. That would be painful and could result in a nasty bruise. The worry that had gripped me since I'd looked into Peter's blank face eased a little.

I scanned the area where I'd seen the two faint trails through the dirt. It extended several feet. Dragging the body that far would take strength. I still didn't think Miss Miller could do it, but everyone else in the house was sturdy and healthy enough to manage, especially if they had a burst of adrenaline running through their system.

I righted the chaise lounge and put it back, then plucked at the front of my dress to circulate the humid air around me. I strolled through the rest of the paths without discovering anything else. I went to the billiard room, which felt like a cool dark cave after the bright overheated atmosphere of the conservatory, thinking I might find Jasper there again.

He wasn't in sight, but Captain Inglebrook, his mouth set in a line as straight as his thin mustache, was poised over the billiard table as he concentrated on aligning his cue stick. I paused in the doorway until he took the shot. The billiard balls clicked, and one dropped neatly into the net at the far end of the table.

"Excellent shot," I said, and he turned at the sound of my voice.

"Hello, Miss Belgrave. Care to join me?"

CHAPTER FIFTEEN

I walked into the billiard room. "No, I can only stay for a moment, Captain. Are you going on the picnic to the ruin this afternoon?"

Inglebrook propped his hip against the edge of the billiard table. "I'll be delighted to accompany you."

"Everyone is going, I believe."

"Nevertheless, your presence will make it all the more enchanting."

I leaned against the table, mirroring his posture, and crossed my arms. "Are you ever serious?"

"Life is far too serious as it is. I bring a little light, a little laughter, a little relief from the tediousness. You're shaking your head," he said. "Don't you agree that we all need a respite from the grim daily routine?"

"No, I wasn't shaking my head about that. I was thinking about how different you are from Inspector Longly. It seems an odd match for friendship."

"Lucas Longly is a long-standing friend"—he paused, and I knew he was teasing me in some way because of his mischievous look—"as well as a distant relative. Didn't you know?"

So, Gwen hadn't had the full story about the two men. Her letter that drew me to Parkview mentioned they were friends, but not relatives. "No. Inspector Longly doesn't speak about himself much."

"He doesn't. Typical British self-effacement. We're cousins removed. Several times removed," he clarified. "We've known each other since we were in our prams."

"Like Gwen and Peter and I." That situation explained what seemed to be a distant relationship between the two men. I could see how the diligent inspector and the blithe captain might not have much in common.

Inglebrook walked around the table and lined up for another shot. "Are you sure you won't join me?"

"No, I'm afraid I can't at the moment. Perhaps Gigi will join you again today as she did last evening. Who won last night?"

"We didn't play."

"You didn't? But Gigi said you spent all afternoon here playing billiards."

"Yes, that's true. She didn't know how to play. I was teaching her."

"I see."

Gigi knew how to play billiards as well as I did, but I was sure that letting Captain Inglebrook show her how to properly hit a billiard ball involved the captain placing his arms around her.

"She was a quick study, though." Inglebrook squinted at the billiard balls and inched to the left.

"Soon we were practicing some advanced maneuvers."

"I bet she was," I murmured as he hit the ball with the cue stick. The clatter of the balls knocking against each other covered my words.

Inglebrook watched the balls until they stopped rolling. "I'm glad Gigi and I were together. It made it so much simpler. It would be disturbing if Lucas had to suspect a relative."

Father sat at the long table in the library with books, maps, and notebooks scattered around him. He was not a neat worker. I'd been surprised at the transformation in his study at Tate House after Sonia had moved in. Somehow she'd convinced him to keep his desk clear, something I'd never been able to do, but here at Parkview he'd reverted to his old style of working. With all the upheaval around Payne's death, it was comforting to see Father surrounded by bookish clutter.

I set a cup of tea beside him. It was only when the cup clinked in the saucer that he looked up. "Oh hello, Olive. I didn't see you there."

"I thought you might like a cup of tea."

"Thank you, my dear. I did just have lunch—Sonia always sees to it that I eat," he said as he picked up the cup. "But one can never turn down a cup of tea."

I pulled out the chair beside him and gestured to his stacks of books and handwritten notes. "How's it coming along?"

"Excellent. Parkview has some wonderful resources. Leo doesn't mind what I borrow from the library, but it's nice to have it all at my fingertips instead of walking back and forth from Tate House." He pushed his spectacles further up his nose and turned fully toward me. "What is the situation with Peter?"

"For the moment, not good, I'm afraid." I kept my idea that Peter had stumbled over the chaise to myself. I had no proof of what happened, and I didn't want to create false hope.

Father took a sip of his tea, then said slowly, "This work you've been doing in London—it's rather unconventional, but your experience may be exactly what's needed to help Peter. Things often work out that way. Think of Esther . . . 'for such a time as this.'"

I already felt the weight of everyone's expectation pushing down on me, which was entirely enough pressure without comparisons to Biblical figures. "I don't think I'm in that category," I said. I'd wanted to succeed with my first few cases so badly so I could continue living on my own. I hadn't realized my accomplishments would lead to such expectations. "But don't worry, I'm doing all that I can to help Peter. In fact, I wanted to chat with you for a moment about last evening."

"Nothing unusual happened, as far as I know." He waved his hand at a stack of books on the other side of the table. "I worked my way through those reference books while you young people were at the maze. Sonia brought me tea, which we had here together, and then we retired upstairs to our room, where she read aloud to me until it was time to dress for dinner. She insists that I not spend all day reading." He tapped his hand on the open pages in front of him. "She says my eyes need rest and that I have a tendency to overdo it."

"Which is probably true," I conceded, even though I still bristled at the thought of Sonia arranging Father's schedule. However, Father's health was much improved, so I couldn't argue too much. "What did she read to you?"

"A cracking good crime novel, *Murder at Castle Colfax*. We're a little over halfway through it. It's quite twisty, and I'm afraid I have no idea who the culprit is."

"I've read that book. I agree." I didn't say anything more. One of the downsides of being a discreet problem solver was that I couldn't share some of the things I'd learned about interesting people and situations, even with those closest to me. "And you were there until you came down for dinner?"

"Yes," Father said as he removed his handkerchief and polished his glasses.

Well, that marked Sonia off my list of potential suspects. Father wouldn't lie for her. I was completely sure of it.

Father said, "I did drift off for a bit. I completely missed chapter twelve, and Sonia had to reread it to me. Perhaps she's right about me working too hard." He chuckled.

I'd been halfway out of my chair, but I dropped back into it. "You fell asleep?"

"Yes. I don't like to admit it, but Sonia is right that I

overdo it. You wouldn't think mental work could tire you, but it does."

"Oh, I agree." I patted him on the shoulder and took his cup. "I'll let you get back to it," I said and left the room, my thoughts spinning. I couldn't mark Sonia off my list after all.

CHAPTER SIXTEEN

*C*ormont Hill was the highest point for miles around, which was why the powerful medieval Cormont family had chosen it for the location of their castle. Unfortunately, their castle and their power had the same fate—both had crumbled. The Cormont family had petered out in the early seventeen hundreds, and by then their castle had fallen into disrepair as well. All that remained of Cormont Castle were several walls of various heights, the tallest with gothic arched windows.

Aunt Caroline had divided up the houseguests and had those of us with motors help transport everyone. Uncle Leo and Father had stayed behind, but everyone else was in attendance. Jasper and I were the last to arrive. His motor was still being repaired in Upper Benning, so I'd driven the Morris. Even if I hadn't known how to reach the hill, Deena's bright red motor parked at the base of the footpath was visible for miles around. As I brought the Morris to a stop beside it, Deena hailed us from halfway up the hill, but we were too far away to hear her words. Beside her, Captain Inglebrook stood with a hand outstretched, waiting to help Deena over a rocky portion of the path, his silk scarf flapping in the breeze. Gwen had ridden with Deena to show her the way to Cormont Hill and was farther up the path. She paused and gave us a wave, then continued on.

I nodded to Ross, who was now in his chauffeur garb. He'd been crouched down, examining the moss that clung to the shady side of one of the large boulders that dotted the landscape. He'd driven Aunt Caroline, Miss Miller, and Sonia in the estate's saloon motor. He had his own picnic lunch waiting for him, spread out on the bonnet of the saloon.

Jasper called out, "Good afternoon, Ross," and hefted the last picnic basket out of the Morris.

Ross removed his cap and returned the greeting.

"Find any interesting plants?" I asked as I started for the path.

"Possibly. The moss is an unusual color."

"Interesting. You might have to take a bit of it back to Parkview."

"That I might," he said as we passed him and walked up the path. I was sure he'd eat lunch and then examine all the plants within walking distance. He'd probably return to Parkview with several cuttings for the greenhouse.

Jasper transferred the picnic basket to his other hand and pulled a telegram out of his pocket. "This came for you shortly before we gathered for this outing. I told

Brimble I'd give it to you. I didn't think you'd want everyone to see it."

I ripped it open. "And you didn't mention it before?"

"As soon as we were settled in your motor, you launched into your list of what you'd been doing."

"I suppose that's true," I said. "I didn't want to forget anything. I need to jot down all the details. There's something about seeing each piece of information in black and white on a piece of paper that helps it stick in my brain. Sorry I dominated the drive."

"No need to apologize. You were quite succinct." Jasper tilted his head to the telegram I'd skimmed. "Unlike that telegram."

It was indeed long for a telegram, but there was a lot of information to convey.

"Yes, but worth every penny. It's from Boggs. He says Vincent Payne, Simon Adams, and Sonia Bernard —that was her maiden name—did live in Clifton Green. Simon's name is listed on the cenotaph in the village, and the village postmistress says Sonia and Simon ran away and married without the approval of Sonia's father. Sonia never returned to the village, and her father moved to Hastings." I folded the telegram and put it in the pocket of my dress. "At least we know that much of her story is true."

"I had some success with my inquiries this afternoon as well," Jasper said.

"Oh, that's speedy. I thought it might take days." We'd reached the steeper section of the climb, which meant I had to take large strides to keep up with Jasper's longer ones.

"I was able to get in touch with my friend, who happens to owe me money from a card game. He was more than willing to make a special trip to locate a few files and pass on some general information."

"And in exchange, you forgave his debt. Thank you, Jasper. I'll pay you back."

"That's not necessary. It's for Peter," he said as we rounded the switchback turn and paused. A few more feet, and we'd be at the top. Jasper wasn't even winded from the climb, but I was glad for a moment to catch my breath. I turned away from the crown of the hill and looked in the opposite direction at Parkview, which glowed a warm gold against the patchwork brown and beige of the empty flowerbeds around it.

Jasper spoke quietly as he adjusted the brim of his hat to shade his eyes. "I was able to confirm Payne and Adams were in the same platoon, which was almost completely wiped out. *Payne*"—Jasper made quote marks in the air—"survived, along with a man named Thaddeus Lessing."

I turned to him. "Perhaps Mr. Lessing—no?"

Jasper shook his head. "Lessing survived that battle but died in nineteen eighteen. Pneumonia."

"Oh. Well, at least now we know parts of Sonia's story—and Mr. Payne's—were true. I just wish Father hadn't drifted off to sleep yesterday afternoon. What an inconvenient time for a nap. If he'd given Sonia an alibi, I'd have believed it."

"Do you really think Sonia was involved in Mr. Payne's death?"

"She's resourceful and ruthless. I don't care what she says about Mr. Payne promising to leave quietly at the end of the party. He *was* a threat to her."

Gwen appeared above us on the path. "There you are. We're waiting for you. You have the rest of the sandwiches."

We followed Gwen up the last turn of the path and emerged into the flat open space at the top of the hill. The full force of the wind smacked us, and I clamped my hat on my head. Aunt Caroline, Miss Miller, and Sonia were seated on a blanket in a sheltered corner created by the intersection of two crumbling walls, which were only a few feet high. Gigi sat on a rock a little distance from them, bent over as she tried to light a cigarette in the blustery air.

On the opposite side of the clearing, a single wall of the castle still stood almost intact. Two stories of pointed gothic windows, empty of glass, looked out over the countryside and framed the beautiful rolling hills, which were a patchwork of brown and muted greens crisscrossed with dry stone walls. In the distance blurry white dots, a flock of sheep, moved lazily across a pasture. Deena and Captain Inglebrook stood next to each other at one window, the wind tugging at their clothes. Deena had changed into one of the sporty new Chanel tweed suits. A feather curved down from her toque to her cheek, emphasizing the elongated shape of her face.

A few feet beyond the wall, the ground fell away in

a sheer drop. There was something about the partially intact wall and window that overlooked the view that drew everyone to it. It was always the first place people went when they arrived at the top of the hill, and we were no different. Jasper, Gwen, and I joined Deena and Inglebrook at the window. Deena pointed. "Look over there on the other side of the ravine. Isn't that Peter?"

I shaded my eyes and spotted Peter's dark hair and lean form. He was nimbly navigating the steep trail that dropped down to the base of the gorge.

Deena leaned out the window and swept her arm back and forth. "Yoo-hoo!" Her enthusiastic wave caused her to overbalance, and she tilted out the window toward the ravine.

CHAPTER SEVENTEEN

*C*aptain Inglebrook caught Deena's elbow and drew her back. "Careful there. That's quite the drop. Wouldn't want you to fall."

Deena smiled and put a hand on the lapel of his coat. "I know you'd never let anything like that happen to me."

"Well, I certainly couldn't let a lady tumble down the hill right beside me."

Deena turned her attention back to the view. "What happened to Peter? I don't see him anymore."

"He saw us," Jasper said. "He'll make his way over."

Aunt Caroline called to us. I picked my way across the rubble-strewn field behind Gwen, still holding my hat on my head until I reached the sheltered corner.

"Whew." The wind had tugged Gwen's fair hair out of the knot at the nape of her neck. She tucked the long strands behind her ears. "I'm glad these old walls can still block the wind." She dropped down onto the blanket beside Miss Miller. "Jasper's brought the rest of the sandwiches."

"Thank you, Jasper," Aunt Caroline said as he set down the picnic basket.

I felt Sonia's intense gaze on me. She sent me a questioning look, and I gave a tiny shake of my head to indicate I'd found nothing conclusive. Sonia seemed to shrink into herself, her normally stiff posture collapsing.

Miss Miller hadn't noticed our silent exchange or the change in Sonia's bearing. "It's so nice to have a man about," Miss Miller said with a smile at Jasper, then she sighed. "I do so miss dear Winston. He would have loved the view here. And he was so good at seeing to things—now I have to sort out the household accounts and financial matters." She pressed a hand into the blanket and leaned toward Aunt Caroline, speaking across Sonia. "Do you know the butcher insists I owe him five pounds. *Five pounds!* I know that's not right. Winston wouldn't have stood for it. Mr. Johnson—the butcher, you know—wouldn't have argued with Winston. It is difficult to be a woman and deal with tradespeople."

"Oh, pish." Deena tucked her skirt under her knees as she settled on the blanket. "You don't need a man for that. I deal with tradesmen all the time. You just have to tell them what's what and not take any guff."

"I don't think I could do that," Miss Miller said, her eyes round.

Sonia nibbled on a sandwich, her gaze focused on the blanket. She didn't seem to be listening to the conversation going on around her. Her face still had the same strained quality it had earlier, and I felt a tug of sympathy for her—something I never thought I'd feel. I'd have to get her alone for a few moments and tell her that Jasper and I were making progress, but be sure to keep it in vague terms.

Deena reached for a sandwich. "Just be firm. My Uncle Jason had that same attitude—that women couldn't handle money. If my poor cousin Bobby hadn't died in the war, Uncle Jason would have left everything to Bobby simply because Bobby was a man." Deena waved her sandwich at Gwen. "You remember Bobby. You can't say he would have been a better manager than me."

Gwen hesitated. "I didn't know him all that well."

I did remember Bobby Stanton. He was a jolly, happy-go-lucky young man with curly reddish hair, who always had lemon drops in his pockets. He hadn't been sober-minded in the least. If he'd inherited Jason Stanton's fortune, I imagined he'd have spent it with abandon, just as Deena was—except Bobby would probably throw elaborate parties and invite everyone. Deena had a tendency to spend her money only on herself. Gwen glanced at me out of the corner of her eye, a silent plea to extricate her from the conversation. Gwen hated to be critical of anyone—well, except for Inspector Longly. She seemed to have no qualms about that.

Before I could speak, Aunt Caroline thumped down another plate of sandwiches. "Let's not speak ill of the dead. Whatever his qualities in the financial arena would have been, the poor boy died an honorable death in service to his country. Let's not belittle him."

Deena dropped her gaze and brushed crumbs from her skirt. "I didn't mean to sound disapproving. I miss him more than anyone." Miss Miller tilted her head in an inquiring manner and Deena explained, "He and I were the only cousins on my mother's side."

"Indeed," Miss Miller murmured. "Well, you young women are so independent-minded, like my Aunt Ethel. She had an interesting life. Such adventures! She traveled the world—"

Aunt Caroline offered the plate of cream cakes, diverting Miss Miller from launching into the biography of her aunt. Gwen said quickly, "You were right, Mother, it's very pleasant up here in the shelter of the wall with the sun shining."

"You could almost forget it's November," I said.

The conversation turned to the vagaries of the weather and upcoming plans for bridge parties. With Aunt Caroline guiding the conversation, we avoided any mention of Payne or murder. The topic of the history of Cormont Castle came up, and as we finished our tea, Gwen gave an entertaining summary of the family's history, which included a lingering ghost.

"Are you sure you won't have a sandwich?" Aunt Caroline asked Gigi, proffering the almost empty plate. Gigi had been sitting a little distance away, smoking as she watched Captain Inglebrook and Deena. They'd sat side by side a little apart from our group. She stubbed out her cigarette. "Thank you, but no. I'm going to wander around and find a quiet place to have a rest in the sun," she said with a steady gaze on Captain Inglebrook.

Her intent gaze must have communicated something to Inglebrook. He was on his feet in an instant. "Wonderful. I'll join you." Gigi slipped her arm through his elbow and they strolled off.

I thought Deena would have scrambled up and gone with them, but she'd just taken a slice of cake and was chewing the first bite.

Sonia put her plate down. "I believe a brisk walk is what I need as well." She marched away at a quick pace, passing Gigi and Inglebrook as they ambled along.

Aunt Caroline stacked the empty plates but put aside some sandwiches and cakes for Peter. "I brought my charcoals. I believe I'll do a quick sketch of Parkview." She nodded to the estate in the distance. She went to a break in the walls and settled herself on a tumbled stone, her back to us. Deena gulped down the cake, then set off in the same direction Gigi and Inglebrook had gone. They'd ducked through a gap in the wall on the side of the ruin that opened onto a short stretch of flat, open land at the top of the hill.

Miss Miller leaned back against the wall. "I believe I'll just rest here in the sun." She folded her hands across her waist and closed her eyes.

Gwen dusted her fingers and tilted her head toward the tall wall with the windows. Jasper and I followed her across the field. She leaned against one of the windowsills, her back to the strong breeze that swept across the ravine. "I have Mr. Payne's movements." She took a piece of paper from her pocket and unfolded it.

"Excellent," I said.

"It all seems fairly straightforward," Gwen said. "Mr. Payne arrived around midmorning on Thursday and spent most of that day with Father, discussing maps." She pointed the paper at me. "Which reminds me. I spoke to Father before we left for the picnic. He met Mr. Payne at his club. Another club member who'd bought a map from Mr. Payne, old Mr. Carsley, introduced him to Father. Gave Mr. Payne a glowing recommendation, and Father invited him—Mr. Payne, that is —to Parkview on the spot."

"So, no connection there." Disappointment darted through me. I'd hoped that Payne's invitation had hinged on a relationship that would give us a link to another guest, but that wasn't the case. I shook off the dispirited feeling. "We'll just have to keep searching. There must be a connection somewhere."

"Right." Gwen went back to her list. "After he and Father finished in the study, Mr. Payne joined us for lunch. Deena and I left for the village, and while we were gone, he suggested a walk in the woods with Gigi."

"And we know how that turned out," I said.

"Yes, then we were all together for dinner and music later that evening."

I mentally penciled in his brief talk with Sonia in the courtyard before dinner on Thursday, but I didn't add it to Gwen's list.

"On Friday," Gwen continued, "Mr. Payne breakfasted late and then went on the house tour with Mother. Afterward, Mr. Payne stayed behind while we all went to the maze."

I said, "He went to the library to look at the photographs from when Parkview was a hospital."

Gwen took a pencil out of her pocket and added a note.

"At least I assume that's what he did," I added. "Aunt Caroline mentioned the photos, and he headed to the library as soon as the tour ended."

Gwen tapped the page with the pencil. "He joined us for tea when we returned from the maze, then he went up to his room. Fillmore served as his valet that evening, and he says he helped Mr. Payne dress and was dismissed shortly before seven. Brimble saw Mr. Payne come downstairs a little after seven and go down the passageway to the conservatory."

Gwen flipped the page over and consulted a new list. "Now for last evening. Brimble was in and out of the entry hall as he oversaw preparations in the drawing room as well as in the dining room. This is the order he remembers everyone arriving. Mother and Father were early—before seven—and went to the drawing room. They don't like a guest to arrive to an empty room. Mr. Payne came down and went into the conservatory. A few minutes later Miss Miller arrived and went directly to the drawing room. Next were Gigi, Captain Inglebrook, and Deena. Deena went to the sitting room while Gigi and Captain Inglebrook went to the drawing room."

"I'd forgotten my lighter," a voice said, and we

turned to peer out of the window. Deena was picking her way along the ledge above the ravine.

Gwen held out a hand through the window. "Gracious, Deena, what are you doing over there?"

"Exploring a bit." Deena didn't take Gwen's hand but continued placing one foot directly in front of the other. "I have excellent balance." She wobbled a bit, extended one arm over the sheer drop as she steadied herself, then took the last few steps and hopped up to the windowsill. She swung her legs over so that she was sitting beside Gwen. "See? Nothing to it. Are we trying to figure out who murdered Mr. Payne? I'll play."

Gwen frowned at her. "It isn't a game. The inspector thinks Peter was involved, and we're trying to prove he wasn't."

"Sorry," Deena said, but she didn't look contrite at all. "I want to help. I went into the sitting room to fetch my lighter. Someone had left a magazine on the sofa, and it had the most divine dress on the cover. I sat down and flipped through the whole thing."

Gwen jotted that down, then went on, "Peter came down next and went to the conservatory as he usually does. Sonia and your father came down next to last, Olive, closer to seven thirty."

"Father said Sonia was reading to him until it was time to dress for dinner."

Gwen made another note on her page. "And finally, you, Olive."

"And that's when Deena met me in the hall and dragged me into the conservatory." I turned to Deena. "When did you go into the conservatory?"

"No idea. I finished with the magazine and thought it would be fun to bring Mr. Quigley down to the conservatory, so I popped along there to see if it was empty, and—well, you know what happened then."

"Right," I said.

Gwen folded the paper. "How I wish I'd been ready early, but I stepped on my hem as I was getting dressed, and it had to be sewn back up before I could leave."

Jasper, who'd been listening with his eyes closed and his face tilted up to the sun, opened his eyes. "Why did Mr. Payne go into the conservatory?"

We all looked at each other.

"Houseguests would normally go to the drawing room," he said. "Why the conservatory?"

"You mean, was it a spur of the moment decision, or had he arranged to meet someone there?" I asked.

"Yes. He'd visited the conservatory earlier," Jasper said. "Perhaps he wanted to look at the flowers and plants again?"

"He didn't show any interest in them during the tour," Deena said. "He stayed by the fountain and didn't stroll around with us while Lady Caroline told us about the rare plants."

Gwen said, "If Mr. Payne was meeting someone there . . ."

Deena jumped down from the windowsill, her face excited. "Find out who it was, and perhaps you'll find his murderer."

Gwen looked over Jasper's shoulder. "There's Peter." She shoved the paper and pencil in her pocket and went to meet him, but she paused after only a few steps. "Peter, what happened?"

Peter was walking with his hands held out from his sides in an awkward manner. His tweed jacket was torn at the shoulder seam, and a thin line of blood trailed down his cheek from a scrape on his forehead over his bruised eye.

Gwen hurried over and handed him her handkerchief. "Did you fall?"

Peter took the scrap of fabric gingerly. The palms of his hands were scraped and scratched. "I was pushed."

CHAPTER EIGHTEEN

*P*eter dabbed at the gash over his eyebrow with Gwen's handkerchief.

She looked from Peter to the tea things still spread on the blanket. "We don't have any water to clean these cuts. We brought the tea in thermoses."

"It's only a few scratches," Peter said.

"But the one on your forehead is bleeding quite a lot."

"That always happens with head wounds," Peter said. "I promise you, it's nothing."

With a glance at Aunt Caroline, who was still sketching with her back to us and hadn't noticed the commotion going on behind her, Gwen lowered her voice. "Are you sure someone pushed you?"

While they were speaking, I swiveled around, scanning the open area. Miss Miller was no longer sleeping in the sun. She must have woken and gone for a walk, and no one else had returned from their rambles except Deena.

Peter refolded the handkerchief to a clean spot and pressed it to the cut. "Absolutely sure. I may have had a little trouble with my memory the other day, but when someone gives you a solid knock on your back, there's no question about what happened, especially when it sends you tumbling over the edge of the path."

Gwen put a hand to her chest. "Into the ravine?"

"Yes. But there were a few sturdy bushes in the undergrowth near the trail. I was able to grab one and pull myself back onto the path.

"Oh, Peter," Gwen said. "How *ghastly*. Oh, and your other hand is worse," she said and caught his free hand, turning it up so she could examine the scrapes on his palm.

"Did you see who it was?" Jasper asked as he offered Peter a clean handkerchief.

Peter pulled his hand away from Gwen, clearly impatient with her fussing. "No. I was too occupied with not plunging several hundred feet."

"Understandable. Did you hear anything?" Jasper asked. "Perhaps in the moment or two before you were pushed?"

"I thought I heard someone on the path behind me. I assumed it was someone from your picnic party who'd come down to say hello and walk with me the rest of the way as I came up here. I was turning to see who it was, but I wasn't quick enough."

Gigi ambled up the path and called out a greeting. She was alone.

"Where's Captain Inglebrook? Did you outpace him?" I asked as she joined us.

"He wanted to see some sort of rock formation, but it was simply too far away. I told him to go on. I'm sure he'll be along in a moment."

"How long ago was it that you and Captain Inglebrook separated?"

Gigi's forehead crinkled into a frown. "I have no idea. I took my time coming back." Peter turned his head, and she saw the gash on his head. "Goodness," she said. "What happened to you?"

Peter said, "A slip of the foot."

"On the trail coming up from the ravine? You're a lucky man."

"So it would appear," Peter said. Gigi didn't seem to notice the irony in his tone.

About a quarter of an hour later, Jasper and I were in the Morris on our way back to Parkview. Gwen had insisted that she and Peter go down Cormont Hill immediately and have Ross take them back to Parkview so Peter's scratches could be cleaned properly. Aunt Caroline, after tutting over Peter's cuts and scrapes, had stayed behind. Once Ross dropped Gwen and Peter at Parkview, he'd return to pick up Aunt Caroline, Sonia, and Miss Miller. Peter wanted to keep the incident quiet. He didn't want to worry Aunt Caroline or Uncle Leo—or increase their already worried state. He convinced Deena not to share the news that he'd been pushed, but I hoped that after Gwen patched him up, she could convince Peter to find Inspector Longly and report what had happened.

A horn blast sounded behind us as the red Alfa Romeo swept by. Deena waved from the driver's seat as she bumped along on the grassy verge of the road. Captain Inglebrook and Gigi were squished together in the front seat beside her. Deena whipped the motor back into the lane and accelerated away. Seconds later, the little red motor swept off the road again to avoid a pothole, then jerked back into the lane.

Jasper said, "I'm glad I accepted your offer of a lift. I don't think my nerves could stand an afternoon drive with Deena."

"She may not be the best driver, but she certainly has the best motor. And that's what's important to Deena." I navigated around the pothole at a more sedate speed, then eased off the gas. I didn't want to arrive at Parkview too quickly. We had things to discuss. "It seems anyone could have pushed Peter, except for you, me, and Gwen."

"I agree. We were the only ones who didn't leave the ruin," Jasper said. "The question is, why would someone do that?"

I gripped the steering wheel tighter. "If something were to happen to Peter before he remembered what happened in the conservatory . . ."

"Yes, it could mean the murderer might never be discovered." Jasper settled his hat more firmly on his head as the breeze kicked up. "I believe I'll have to stick with Peter from now on."

"That sounds like an excellent idea."

We spent the rest of the drive talking through everyone's movements on Cormont Hill, but we didn't work out any new solution to who might have pushed Peter. As soon as we arrived back at Parkview and the picnic baskets were unloaded from the Morris, I handed off my hat, gloves, and coat and went directly to the library. Jasper followed me. "I thought you were going to stay with Peter," I said.

"I'm sure Gwen won't let him out of her sight for a while. I assume you're going to peruse the photo albums?"

"Of course. If they interested Mr. Payne, we should look at them."

"I agree." Jasper paused at the library door to allow me to precede him into the room.

Father, who was seated at the long table surrounded by stacks of books, lifted his pen and glanced up. "Hello, Olive. Jasper. How was the picnic? Is Sonia back as well?"

"She should be here shortly. Don't mind us. We're just after one thing."

Father went back to his writing as we went to the bookcases. "Aunt Caroline said the albums were on the lower shelf by the staircase. Here they are." Several albums tilted against each other, and I pulled them all out.

I stacked them in Jasper's arms, and he carried them to a small table on the far side of the library from Father so we wouldn't disturb him. We each picked an album.

A quick glance was enough to show whether or not the pictures had been taken during the war. The photos in the album I'd opened were too early to contain anything from the time during the war, but I couldn't help looking at a few of the snapshots. Gwen had received the Brownie camera as a Christmas present, and she'd been keen on photography for several years.

"Look, here's one of you and Peter when you were both about ten. You look like you were up to quite a bit of mischief." The picture showed Jasper with his rumpled fair hair glowing in the sun and dark-haired Peter standing in the garden. "And here's one of all of us playing doubles."

"I seem to remember you girls beat us soundly that afternoon."

I closed the album reluctantly. "Let's not get distracted. We can come back and browse through these later. If we don't stay focused, we could be here all afternoon."

"Yes, you're right."

I picked up the next album. I could tell from the shirtwaists and long narrow skirts Aunt Caroline wore in the photos that we were close to the right time period. "Look, there's one of Deena helping to sort bedding as we prepared Parkview." There were a few photos of Gwen and me rolling bandages, but then the photos reverted to a few years prior, when Gwen and I were several years younger. "These are out of order," I said as I flipped quickly through several pages. "Here we are. This is the mahogany room being readied for patients. And this one of the portrait gallery is exactly as Payne described it." Tables ranged around the room with games, books, magazines, and crossword puzzles.

I turned to the next page, expecting to see images of patients, doctors, and nurses, but it was blank with empty spaces where pictures had been. The next one was blank too. And the next. "Why, they're gone," I said as I flipped faster through a few more pages. All the little black photo mounting corners that had held the pictures in place were empty. Dark squares stood out against the faded pages, showing where the photographs had once been. "Someone's taken them all."

Jasper frowned. "What? All of them?"

"Yes, after the pictures of the preparations to turn Parkview into a hospital, there's nothing. Not a single photograph."

A quick look through the rest of the albums showed they didn't contain any photos from during the war.

We were hunched over the table, our heads bent. Jasper looked sideways at me, his hands braced on the table. "There could only be one reason someone would remove all of them—someone was worried about what was in the photos."

I straightened and closed the heavy album with a thump. "But was it Mr. Payne who removed them, or someone else? And where are they now?"

"Burnt, I imagine." Jasper straightened and glanced at the fireplace, where the flames were flickering.

"That's horrible. What a loss! Those might have

been the last photos taken of some of the men who didn't survive the war. To destroy that record—it's—well, it's like destroying an archive."

"Terrible," Jasper agreed, "but a small thing compared to murder."

CHAPTER NINETEEN

*U*nlike the incident at the ruin when Peter was pushed, we weren't able to keep the missing photographs quiet. I rang up the police station in Nether Woodsmoor, and Inspector Longly arrived with several constables. They were currently searching every fireplace in Parkview, something that couldn't be kept hush-hush. The search was the main topic of conversation during afternoon tea. The ladies, who were better represented than the men, had gathered around the tea table, but Uncle Leo sat away from the group, nestled in an armchair behind his raised newspaper. Jasper went off to try to convince Peter to report being pushed off the trail. Captain Inglebrook stood at the window, his gaze focused on the gardens.

Sonia came in carrying her needlepoint and took a seat. Aunt Caroline paused in pouring the tea. "Cecil's not coming?"

Sonia slipped a thimble on and arranged her thread.

"No, he's at a particularly tricky part and wants to finish. I arranged for his tea to be sent to him there."

Aunt Caroline resumed pouring. "He's always at a tricky point." Aunt Caroline handed the saucer to Gwen, who was passing the cups around.

Gwen handed the cup to Miss Miller. "He's just the same as you when you are involved in a painting."

Aunt Caroline's expression telegraphed her disapproval at the comparison, but she didn't pursue the topic. She turned to Miss Miller. "What were you saying earlier, Marion?"

Miss Miller blinked. "What?"

"About the missing photographs," Aunt Caroline added.

Miss Miller replaced her cup in the saucer. "Oh, yes. I don't see why the police are making such a fuss about the photographs."

"It means Mr. Payne's death must have something to do with his time here at Parkview during the war," Gwen said promptly.

She was eager to get out the news that there was another possible explanation for Payne's death besides Peter having an episode.

"You mean the time he mentioned when we toured the house? When he was here as a patient?"

"Exactly," Gwen said. She passed a plate of biscuits. "You were here then, Miss Miller. Do you remember him?"

Miss Miller fumbled with the biscuit, dropping crumbs into her lap. "No, I didn't recognize him at all."

"I didn't realize you worked here at Parkview

during that time, Miss Miller. Did you have nursing experience?" I took a biscuit and passed the plate to Gigi, who was reclining on the settee with one leg curled up under her.

"Heavens, no," Miss Miller said. "I only helped out, reading to the patients and doing jigsaw puzzles occasionally. Early on during the war, I dropped in a few times a week, but the men preferred the prettier, younger girls to me. I wasn't as much in demand as they were. And then poor Winston broke his hip, and I had to attend to him. That was in nineteen fifteen, I believe. Such a trying time. Winston was cranky and the news was so terrible all the time." She put down her biscuit without taking a bite. "It was so bleak then. I was never able to return to Parkview. Poor Winston required all my attention." Miss Miller nodded at Sonia. "The only person here with any nursing experience is our clever Sonia, I believe. I don't see how you did it," Miss Miller said to Sonia. "Winston was grumpy— extremely grumpy—not at all his usual demeanor."

Sonia had accepted a cup of tea but had placed it on the table beside her instead of drinking it. She'd continued to work on her needlepoint, but the light glinting on the needle showed the trembling of her hands. However, her voice was smooth as she said, "Patients are often not at their best. The pain makes them testy. It's best to just pretend they're not rude or whiney."

"Still, it must have been so difficult," Miss Miller said. "At least your surroundings were lovely." Miss Miller gestured with her teacup to the room.

Sonia stabbed the needle into the fabric at an angle to stow it away, then tucked the fabric down between the edge of the chair and her leg. "Oh, I didn't work here as a nurse, only in a hospital in London." She turned slightly to me. "That's how I came to be your father's nurse." She tilted her head toward Aunt Caroline. "When he fell ill, Lady Caroline recommended me."

"Oh, I hadn't realized."

Captain Inglebrook swiveled away from the window. "Well, if Lucas needed another reason to exclude me from his inquiries—and he doesn't, of course," he said with a little laugh, "then that's it. If it's down to something that happened here during the war, that leaves me out of it."

Gigi swung her foot back and forth and looked at him from underneath her lashes. "That makes two of us."

Only Gigi could make a statement like that and have it come off sounding rather suggestive.

Captain Inglebrook raised his eyebrows a fraction, clearly interested in playing along with Gigi's provocative tone. "Indeed?"

"This is my first visit to Parkview as well," Gigi said. "I've never run across Mr. Payne socially, thank goodness."

Aunt Caroline drew a breath to change the topic, but the door opened and Inspector Longly entered. Everyone fell silent.

Aunt Caroline pursed her lips. Clearly, she was in the same camp as Gwen and wasn't happy with the inspector, but her good breeding came through as she spoke into the awkward pause. "Inspector, do join us for a cup of tea."

"Thank you, but I cannot at the moment." He paused halfway across the carpet, then spotted Uncle Leo, who'd lowered his paper. "We've finished our search, Sir Leo. Thank you for cooperating."

"Of course. Can't stand in the way of an investigation. Wouldn't be cricket. Find anything?"

"In the fireplaces, no. But the remnants of some photographs were discovered in the incinerator."

"In the incinerator," Gigi said with a laugh. "How can that be? Wouldn't anything in there be—well, incinerated?"

"Not always, Lady Gina," Longly said. "It depends on where items are inside the central chamber. If they're off to the side, away from the main area where the burning occurs, they can remain intact or fragments of the items can be left behind, which is what we have. The edges of several photographs."

"How can you be sure it was a photograph?" Aunt Caroline asked.

"The gloss on the paper is quite clear. There's no question what the fragments were, and it shows that someone here at Parkview went out of their way to destroy evidence."

Gwen put her saucer down with a snap. "And it's further proof Peter had nothing to do with Mr. Payne's death. Peter was hardly ever here during the war. He was at school, and then fighting," Gwen said in a challenging tone to the room at large, but I knew her comments were directed to Longly.

Longly stared at Gwen a moment, his expression completely shut down. "That may be the case, but it requires further investigation. Sir Leo, it's necessary that I speak to your guests again. The library is occupied. May I have use of your study?"

"Certainly. It's at your disposal." Leo folded his paper. "Shall I go with you now?"

"Yes, that would be helpful," Longly said. "And after that, Miss Belgrave, then Miss Stone, please."

"It's just so frustrating," Gwen said as she plopped down on the sofa beside me in the drawing room after her interview with Longly. I'd already had my turn. I'd told him everything I could about the photo albums, which didn't amount to much more than I'd looked through them and found the photos missing. Gwen kept her voice soft so as not to disturb the other occupants of the drawing room, who were still arranged around the tea tray at the other side of the room, but her voice vibrated with irritation. "Clearly the missing photos are crucial, but Inspector Longly seemed to think they were of no importance."

"I don't think that's true. He did have the house searched for them and he's speaking to each of us about them."

Gwen didn't seem to hear me and continued speaking. "Inspector Longly is the most infuriating man in all of England, no—in all the world."

Gwen was rarely so passionate about anything. "That's quite a strong reaction."

She jerked toward me, her hands fisted. "He refuses to admit that this new evidence of the missing photographs points to someone besides Peter. He doesn't even seem to have taken the photos into account."

I put a hand on her arm. "I'm sure if he could remove Peter from his suspect list, he would, if only for you."

"Well, he doesn't act like that at all," Gwen said, but a blush had crept into her cheeks. She shifted on the cushion. "What more does he need? Peter never came across Mr. Payne when the war was on. Peter wasn't even here when we opened the hospital. He was at school."

"It's a shame there are no records from nineteen fourteen."

"What do you mean?"

"When Aunt Carolyn gave the tour, Mr. Payne mentioned that he had been here in nineteen fourteen. If you had records from the time Parkview served as a hospital, we'd know exactly when Mr. Payne was here. Then if Peter was away during that time . . ."

"It would force Inspector Longly to move away from Peter as a suspect."

I didn't think it would be so clear-cut as that, but before I could point that out, Gwen said, "But of course there are records."

"Weren't all the records moved to London when they moved the hospital?"

Gwen all but bounced on the cushion in her excitement. "No, I don't believe so. I remember there was some discussion about transferring the paperwork, but I don't think it ever happened. It was all boxed up and put away."

"Put away where?"

Gwen smiled. "Where one puts everything that has to be stored away—in the attic."

CHAPTER TWENTY

"*I* should have brought my gloves." I closed a box and moved to the next one. "It's freezing up here."

"Only a few more to go," Gwen said, her head down as she bent over a crate filled with papers.

The attic at Parkview was a huge space crammed with boxes, trunks, rolled rugs, and discarded furniture, but Gwen had strode across the bare, dusty floorboards with confidence to an area just beyond a decrepit pram and pulled a chain attached to a dangling light bulb. With a single-minded focus, she'd already made good progress on the little area she'd selected for us to search, which was bounded by a steamer trunk on one side and a table in the Jacobean style on the other. The stack of boxes she'd already looked through was as high as her shoulder.

"What about the twenty or thirty boxes under the window?"

"We don't need to check those. They're mostly from the nursery."

I turned my back on the attic and its seemingly endless storage capacity and put another box on a rickety straight-backed chair that was missing its cane seat. "We should have informed Inspector Longly that the records might be in the attic. His men should be conducting the search."

Gwen stopped pawing through the crate and looked at me over her shoulder. "When have you ever been one to worry about breaking rules?"

"I don't break rules. I *bend* them occasionally, especially when the rules are ridiculous." I opened the box.

"And it would be ridiculous to wait for Inspector Longly's people to go through all this," Gwen said. "We're expediting things. We can find the relevant files and—what is it?"

"Hospital records." The box I'd opened contained folders with men's names on the tabs along with dates. "From nineteen fifteen, it looks like."

Gwen came over and opened the next box. "Here we go, nineteen fourteen." Her fingers rippled across the tabs. "They're alphabetical. It should be—" Her voice pulsed with excitement. "Right. *Payne, Vincent.*" She splayed the folder open and skimmed through the pages. "He arrived October thirtieth, nineteen fourteen with multiple injuries, including a broken leg. He was put in an empty bed in the mahogany room."

"Yes, that's the room he remembered."

"Peter wouldn't have been here then. He'd have already gone back to school after his mid-term break."

Gwen turned the pages. "This lists Mr. Payne's medication and has the doctors' notes. Looks like it was old Dr. Grimshaw who saw him the most. There was some doubt about his leg and whether or not he'd recover. They thought they might have to amputate at one point, but his wound healed. He left . . . let's see, December eighth. So that leaves Peter completely out of it. He wouldn't have returned for Christmas holiday before then."

"Well, that's good news." I pulled the first file out of the box and scanned the dates.

"What are you doing?" Gwen had taken a step toward the door. "Don't you want to come downstairs with me and show this to Inspector Longly?"

"He's left. When we first came up here, I saw him and his sergeant leaving in the police motor."

"Well, I'll telephone the police station."

"Let me look through the rest of these files now that we have a window of time. We can pull the files of everyone else who was here when Mr. Payne was a patient."

"Oh, excellent idea," Gwen said. "We'll not only give him proof Peter wasn't involved, but we'll give him heaps of other suspects to investigate. In fact, let's give him the name of everyone who was here—patients and staff. There shouldn't be that many patient files. That was fairly early in the war, and Mother hadn't expanded the hospital to include both wings. I'll look for the roster of medical staff. I know mother had one."

I worked my way through the folders, checking the dates. I stacked the ones that matched the dates of Mr.

Payne's stay on the Jacobean table. "I've found a few . . . Benjamin Henry Allan, Carl Cummins, Percival Winston Finton—" I paused over the name *Winston*. It couldn't have been Miss Miller's brother—he would have been too old to have fought in the war, but the name triggered another thought. "Didn't Miss Miller say she volunteered here at Parkview in nineteen fourteen?"

"Yes, she said her brother broke his hip in nineteen fifteen, but she pitched in before that." Gwen tilted her head and looked into the distance. "I don't remember seeing Miss Miller here, but that doesn't mean much. Mother would only let me visit the men in the afternoon at teatime. I don't know all of the people who came and went. I'm sure there's a record of volunteers as well. I'll just have to find it."

I nodded and went back to the files, murmuring their names as I added them to the stack. "Godfrey Rufus Lunn, Charles Robert Stanton, Rodger Scott, Thomas Talmage, and Wesley Godfrey Williams. I think that's the lot. Nine patients in all, besides Mr. Payne. That shouldn't be too difficult."

"Olive, come look at this." Gwen's voice was sharp.

"What's wrong?"

Gwen handed me a crinkled piece of paper. "It was in with the volunteer log. It's a list of people Mother interviewed for positions in the hospital." She tapped a name. "Isn't that Sonia's maiden name? I noticed it because the name *Sonia* caught my eye. Otherwise, I might have skimmed right over it . . ."

I angled the paper to the light to make sure I was

reading the words correctly. "*Sonia Bernard*," I read, then dropped my arms to my side. "Sonia lied. She said she'd never worked here." I jerked the paper back up to the light and searched for a date. "November thirtieth, *nineteen fourteen*."

Sonia had lied to me about being at Parkview. What else had she lied about? Even though Jasper and I had verified portions of the story she'd told, it was impossible to check every bit of it. "Oh, this is dreadful. If Sonia had something to do with Mr. Payne's death—"

My heart ached for Father. If Sonia was responsible for Payne's death, Father would be devastated. He'd been a widower for years and years before he married Sonia. To find out about the bigamy would be terrible, but to discover she was a murderess on top of that—? I shied away from thinking about it. It was too painful.

Gwen put her hand on my arm. "Olive, did you hear what I said? We shouldn't delay. We have to inform Inspector Longly." She looked at her watch. "There's enough time to do it before we have to dress for dinner."

"Yes." I dragged my gaze away from the folders. "Yes, I did. And you're right. Inspector Longly needs to know." No matter how ghastly the situation would be for Father, the police had to know. I handed the paper with the list of interviewees to her. "Will you do it?"

She gave my arm a squeeze. "Of course. I'll use the telephone in Father's study." She turned away, then stopped, her gaze on the files. "Where should we put them?" Gwen asked. "Inspector Longly will want to see them, but I don't want to cart them all down to the study either—that might lead to questions."

I eyed the dusty pile. "We could leave them here. They've been undisturbed for years and years . . ."

"No, I don't like that idea," Gwen said. "Anyone could come up here and have a look. There's no lock on the attic door, and it's obvious where we've been looking." Gwen nodded toward the trail of footprints we'd left in the dust on the floorboards.

"Let's use one of the cupboards behind the wainscoting." It was a storage place Sonia didn't know about.

"Good idea," Gwen said. "I'll take the first half of the alphabet and put them in my room, and you take the others. The whole stack would be too unwieldy for one of us to carry." She gathered up the folders. "I'll see you in the drawing room before dinner."

I picked up the remaining files, tucked them in the box, and followed Gwen, my steps slower than hers as she raced away down the narrow and uncarpeted stairs. I saw two maids on my way to my room, but no guests. I deposited the files in the little cupboard behind the wainscoting in the Oriental room, dusted my hands, and went to look for Aunt Caroline. If I hurried, I could catch her before she went down to the drawing room.

When I stepped into the hallway, I nearly ran into Sonia. "Goodness, Olive, you're coated in dust. What have you been doing?"

"Helping Gwen." I almost hurried around her, but then I stopped. There was nothing to be lost if I asked her about what we'd found. She couldn't do anything to me in the middle of the afternoon in the corridor of the guest rooms at Parkview. Maids were moving back and forth from room to room, preparing garments for guests and carrying hot water for those who preferred to use a hip bath instead of waiting for the bath in each hall, not to mention the guests who were also about, changing for dinner. The corridor might be deserted, but the wing wasn't empty. A shout would bring people running.

I shifted so that I wasn't blocking the light from the wall sconce. I wanted to see her face clearly. "Why did you lie, Sonia?" I asked, my insides twisting. In a distant part of my mind, I noted my physical reaction and almost couldn't believe it. If someone had told me a few weeks ago I'd feel a mix of dread—and regret, I realized—as I confronted Sonia with her lie, I would've thought the person was barmy.

Sonia's brows snapped down into a scowl. "What are you talking about?"

"You *did* come here to Parkview during the war, when Aunt Caroline interviewed you for a nursing job."

CHAPTER TWENTY-ONE

*S*onia drew herself up a few more inches. "I never lied to you. Everything I told you has been the complete truth. You asked me if I'd ever worked here as a nurse. The answer is no. Lady Caroline did invite me here for an interview. A friend who worked here recommended me to Lady Caroline. I came for the interview because my friend said it was an excellent position, better than any she'd had in London. I was on the grounds of Parkview for all of a quarter hour. I traveled from London, met with Lady Caroline, then returned to London the next day."

"But it was when Mr. Payne was here as a patient."

For a moment Sonia looked as if she'd been walking along and missed a step on uneven pavement. "What?"

A door down the corridor opened, and Deena stepped out, dressed head to toe in silver. From her silver comb decorating her hair, to her dangling diamond earrings, to her silver-toned shoes that sparkled with every step, everything she wore shimmered and spoke of opulence. She gave us a nod as she passed. Something pinged in my mind as I watched her walk away, but Sonia's fierce whisper drew my attention back to her.

"I'll thank you not to make unfounded accusations. I had nothing to do with Simon—I mean, Mr. Payne's death, and whether or not I was here at Parkview for a few moments in nineteen fourteen means nothing. Nothing." She turned away, then spun back to face me. "And if you mention this to your father, you'll regret it. I know you think nothing can come between you and him, but I can turn him against you. And if you pursue this, this—slander—against me, I'll convince him you're nothing but a grasping hussy out to cast me in a bad light." Her words were like a physical blow, and I fell back a step. Her nostrils flared as she breathed in. I thought I saw a look of hurt in her eyes for a moment, then it was gone. "I thought I could trust you. Everyone speaks of how generous and loyal you are, but I don't see any evidence of it—none at all."

She jerked open her door and stepped back inside her room. I caught a glimpse of her face as she blew out a breath and transformed her expression into a serene mask. "No, nothing's wrong, Cecil. I decided I do want to wear my shawl tonight . . ." The door clicked softly.

Her ability to abruptly cloak her emotions was disturbing, but part of a nurse's job was to present a calm, confident manner. She must have had lots of practice hiding her true feelings.

I walked slowly down the hall. Could it simply be a coincidence that Sonia was at Parkview when Payne was a patient? Was Sonia being completely honest? She certainly had the strength and determination to do away with Payne, but if Payne's death was linked to something that happened in nineteen fourteen and Sonia was only here at Parkview for a quarter of an hour then, how would she even know Payne was here as well? Unless Aunt Caroline took Sonia on a tour of the hospital and introduced her to some of the patients.

My steps quickened as I went directly to Aunt Caroline's room and tapped on her door. She was seated at her dressing table in her wrapper, her head tilted to one side as she put on an earring. "Hello, Olive." Her gaze met mine in the mirror. "Is something wrong? Is it Peter?" she asked, half rising from the chair.

"No, it's nothing like that." I waved her back down and took a seat on the blanket trunk at the foot of the bed. When we were little, Gwen and I would sit on the trunk and watch her dress before parties, giggling and dreaming of dressing up so elegantly.

I pulled my mind away from the memories. "When you were running the hospital here at Parkview, do you remember interviewing Sonia for a nursing position?"

"Yes, of course. She made a marvelous impression. I thought she'd do an excellent job." Aunt Caroline tipped her head in the opposite direction and attached the other earring. "Why?"

I scrambled for an explanation. "I didn't realize you'd recommended her when Father was ill. I was curious about the whole situation."

Aunt Caroline picked up a comb and smoothed her

hair. "You and your curiosity. It's rather insatiable," she said, but her tone was indulgent.

"But you didn't hire her."

"No, the position I thought I'd need to fill didn't become vacant. The nurse decided to stay on, so I didn't need to hire anyone at that time."

"Did you take Sonia on a tour of Parkview when she was here?"

Aunt Caroline dabbed scent on her wrist. "Of course not. There wasn't time for anything of that sort. It was simply a quarter hour of conversation. We chatted a bit. I went over her references, and then she departed. I was always on the lookout for a good nurse, and she was highly recommended. I never gave tours to the nurses I interviewed. That would happen when they arrived for work."

"I see."

Aunt Caroline replaced the glass bottle on her dressing table. "You'd better run along and get ready. You look quite dusty."

"Yes, I am rather a mess."

I stopped by Gwen's room to tell her that Sonia was not as good a candidate for a suspect as we thought, but Gwen wasn't in her room. Perhaps it had taken longer than she thought to get through to the inspector and she was still on the telephone. I didn't have time to go down and find her, then return upstairs and change for dinner. I'd have to draw her aside tonight and speak to her before dinner. I hoped Longly had been out and she'd had to leave him a message. If he made his way back to Parkview, I'd have to catch him before he interrupted dinner and tell him we'd been mistaken about Sonia.

I raced back to my room, rang for Hannah, and requested she draw me a bath. I was too filthy to just change into my evening gown. I was lost in my own thoughts, not paying much attention to Hannah's chatter as I looked through my jewelry box, until she said something about the color of hair accessories. I put down the string of jet beads and turned. "What was that?"

She'd hooked the hanger with my dress on the Chinese screen and was straightening the sash on the dropped waistline, but she halted her movements at my sharp tone. "I'm sorry, miss. I was just yammering on. I'll be quiet."

"No, what did you say about hair accessories?"

"Just that Miss Lacey has such beautiful things. Imagine having accessories like feathers, jewelry, shoes, and gloves to match every outfit. She has every color in the rainbow in her wardrobe."

"Yes, Deena does have the finest of everything in matching shades."

Hannah went through and turned on the taps in the bath, and I stared at my reflection in the glass without seeing it, my brain cells firing away.

When she turned off the water, I said, "I'll ring for you when I'm done with the bath. I want a good long soak tonight."

"Very good, miss," Hannah said and left me.

Normally, I'd soak in the deep luxurious warm water, but tonight I didn't have time for that. I slipped in and out of the water as quickly as possible and didn't ring for Hannah again. Instead, I left the water standing in the tub, went to the lacquered screen, and took down my evening gown. I slipped the dress over my head. It only had a few buttons on the side, which I could fasten without help. I put on my plain shoes and picked up my gloves.

When I stepped into the corridor, Jasper was coming my direction. "Ah, Olive. I haven't seen you all afternoon."

I grabbed his arm and drew him into the room. I closed the door, and he said, "My, this is unusual. You've never dragged me into your room."

"I have something important to tell you."

"All business, I see." Jasper crossed his arms and leaned against the door.

"The files from the time that Parkview was a hospital were stored here in the attic. Gwen and I have been through them." Jasper straightened, the easy smile leaving his face. I told him what we found and Sonia's explanation of her time at Parkview. "Aunt Caroline confirmed that she interviewed Sonia here, but that it was only a short interview. She didn't take Sonia around Parkview. I don't see how she could have been aware that Mr. Payne was here."

"So, it wasn't an outright lie, but more an oversight —an omission."

"Which can be just as devious . . . but in this case, it appears it doesn't matter."

"I made progress as well—also on the negative

front," Jasper said. "I was able to confirm that Captain Inglebrook didn't serve with Mr. Payne."

"So they weren't known to each other either."

"Right," Jasper said. "It seems we're being quite successful at clearing people but not finding the murderer."

"I do have one more idea. It's a bit odd, and I don't know how it fits in with everything else—in fact, it doesn't seem to fit in with anything, but I'd like to look into it because, well, to be honest, we have nothing else left to do."

"And your tone indicates you're going to be cagey about telling me the specifics."

"I'd rather not until I know for sure. Will you come along and keep watch while I take a quick look around someone's room?"

"Of course. Remember our sobriquet, partners in crime?" Jasper asked, referring to the nickname he'd given us after we uncovered a criminal at Blackburn Hall. "I can't let you break into someone's room without a lookout. That's the first rule of sleuthing."

CHAPTER TWENTY-TWO

*J*asper looked at the card in the nameplate and murmured, "Goodness," but he didn't say anything else.

I tapped on the door and waited. When there was no answer, I went in and closed the door behind me. Mr. Quigley's cage, an enormous rectangular thing, stood in one corner. It was nearly as large as a wardrobe and must have taken two footmen to move it upstairs. He let out a resounding squawk. "Hush, Mr. Quigley," I whispered. "It's only me. You remember me, right? It's Olive."

Mr. Quigley let out a whistle that I was sure could be heard all over the house. A folded black cloth lay between the large cage and the smaller round cage that Deena had used to transport Mr. Quigley for the village shopping trip. I scurried over, twitched the cloth open, and tossed it over the cage. "Sorry, boy." I waited a moment, but he was silent. I hoped he'd settle down for a rest.

I took a deep breath to calm my skittering pulse and went to the wardrobe. It was stuffed so full of dresses that the doors popped open from the pressure of the fabric against them when I released the latch. Rows of shoes filled the base of the wardrobe. I carefully looked over each of them, then searched the other drawers and cupboards, again coming up empty. I removed the cloth from Mr. Quigley's large cage, refolded it, and went to the door.

Jasper, who had been leaning against the wall with his arms crossed, straightened when I emerged. "Any luck?"

"I'll say. They weren't there."

Jasper cocked his head to one side. "You and I have different definitions of lucky."

"No, it's exactly what I needed to know. I'm sure you've noticed how everything Deena wears matches, from her hair ornaments down to her shoes. It's all in a similar shade."

"Yes, she's always well-turned-out."

"Do you recall what she was wearing the night Mr. Payne died?"

"A blue frock, I believe."

"I knew you'd remember. You're good with fashion. Specifically, her gown that night was royal blue. When Longly was talking to us in the drawing room, I noticed Deena's shoes were light blue." I raised my eyebrows.

"I'm afraid I don't follow," Jasper said.

"There are no royal blue shoes in the wardrobe. I don't think she was reading a magazine in the sitting room. She slipped into the conservatory during one of the moments when Brimble wasn't in the entry hall. I think she murdered Mr. Payne and got something on her shoes—probably blood. Once she realized what had happened, she dashed back upstairs to change into another pair of shoes. She must have disposed of the royal blue shoes later."

"And Brimble didn't see her coming back down the second time?" Jasper said, his tone thoughtful as he tested out the idea. "I suppose it could have happened that way. But perhaps she didn't have shoes that exactly matched her dress."

"Jasper, she prides herself on being a fashion plate. She has shoes to match every gown. How could someone who wears perfectly coordinated outfits *not* have a pair of shoes to match that exquisite evening gown? For goodness' sake, she has silver shoes. Of course she'd have a pair of shoes in the same shade as her royal blue dress."

"You're quite passionate about this fashion clue, I see," Jasper said, then hurried on before I could argue. "I'm not belittling it. But why did Deena kill Mr. Payne?"

That was the sticky point. "I'm not sure, but it must have something to do with the time Mr. Payne was a patient here during the war since the photographs were destroyed. Deena volunteered here. Perhaps there was a photograph of Deena and Mr. Payne together. Yes, I bet that's the reason. Remember, I saw a picture of Deena helping to prepare Parkview for patients, but it was out of order in the album. She removed all the other photos but missed that one because it wasn't grouped with the rest of them."

Jasper said, "So she must have taken the other photographs from the album after she killed Mr. Payne—perhaps during the night."

"If we're right and it all links back to the time when Parkview was a hospital, the answer may be in the hospital files. I have some of them in my room." As I spoke, we walked along the hall, speeding by the medieval tapestry and the glass antiquities cabinet. "The rest of the files are in Gwen's room. If we hurry, we can take a look at the ones in my room before we go down." My steps quickened as I closed the distance to my room. "We'll be the last ones to arrive in the drawing room, but we should be able to make it before they go into dinner."

I went to the recessed cupboard and pressed the trim piece. "Gwen found a volunteer log. Perhaps Deena's name is on it."

The cupboard door popped open. Jasper stepped forward. "Allow me." He pulled out the box and set it on the bed, then stepped back and brushed down his sleeves, which were now covered in dust.

"Sorry about that," I said. "Tell Grigsby I'm to blame." I began removing the folders, stacking them on the bed. "These are the files for patients who were here during nineteen fourteen, but I think the volunteer log should be here as well—" I halted, my gaze fixed on the name on the tab of the folder I held.

My sudden stillness caused Jasper to look up from

swatting away a thready cobweb that trialed from his cuff.

"This patient's name was Robert Stanton." My thoughts were coming so quickly that I had to sit down on the edge of the bed. "Robert—Bobby—Stanton."

"Didn't know him," Jasper said with a shake of his head.

"Oh, right. They visited a few times, but you weren't here then. Bobby Stanton was Deena's cousin. Bobby died during the war, and she inherited her uncle's fortune. Remember she told us about it at the picnic? How her uncle thought she wouldn't be able to handle the finances of the inheritance and intended to leave it all to Bobby because he was a man?"

"And from her motor and clothes, it was a large fortune, I gather?"

"Enormous." I opened the folder and skimmed through the information, reading aloud. "Bobby died here on November seventh, nineteen fourteen." I looked up at Jasper. "He was in the mahogany room. That's where Mr. Payne was as well."

Jasper, his hands in his pockets, paced away, then came back, his gaze focused on the floor. "So Vincent Payne was there when Bobby died."

"Perhaps Deena killed Bobby and Mr. Payne saw her do it." I went back to Bobby's file and turned to the last pages. "The notes say Bobby didn't respond to the nurse when she checked on him during her rounds." I picked up Mr. Payne's file and flipped to the page with that date. "Mr. Payne was given morphine that morning, and he was due for another dose at one o'clock. If he was coming around when Mr. Stanton died and he saw what happened . . ."

"But then why did Mr. Payne keep silent all these years?" Jasper reached for Payne's file.

"I don't know. Perhaps Mr. Payne was groggy from the morphine and was in and out of consciousness, not completely aware of what was happening around him. Perhaps he didn't work out what actually happened until later."

Jasper had been scanning the file as I spoke. He snapped it closed. "If nothing else, I think you found the connection between Deena and Mr. Payne."

"Quite." I began shoving the folders back into the box. "Let's leave the files here, hidden behind the wainscoting." Like Sonia, I doubted Deena knew where the hidden cupboards were. "Deena's in the drawing room. I saw her go down earlier. Why don't you keep an eye on her while I telephone Longly?"

Jasper tossed the file in the box. "Oh, no. I'm not leaving you alone for a moment, old bean, now that we know what's what."

"That's sweet of you, but completely unnecessary." I bent down and pushed the trim piece to open the cupboard. "I'm good at taking care of myself."

Jasper picked up the box. "Yes, I've noticed, but perhaps you'll indulge me."

He was hard to resist when he looked at me like that. "All right. We'll stay together."

"Good." He put the box away. "Just give me a moment to clean up before we go downstairs." He went through to the bath, swiping at the new streaks of dust on his sleeves and the lapels of his dinner jacket.

Since I'd only handled the files, not the box, I wasn't as dusty as Jasper was. The sound of running water came from the bath as I wiped my hands on my handkerchief. I went to the mirror of the dressing table to check my appearance.

A metallic click sounded as the door swung open—Hannah returning to help me dress. Why hadn't I locked the door? And Jasper was in my room—well, the adjoining bath, but the door was open—scandalous! The news would be all over the house before the evening was out.

I swiveled around, "Hannah—"

But it was Deena who stepped through the door and closed it smoothly with her elbow, despite being burdened with Mr. Quigley's small cage, which was swathed in a cloth except for the ring at the top where she held it. She wore a stylish cloche, her driving coat with the mink collar, and had the strap of her handbag hooked over her forearm. I took in those details as a hazy background in contrast to the small pistol she held in her hand.

CHAPTER TWENTY-THREE

"**G**ood evening, Olive," she said in a perfectly normal tone of voice as she set the birdcage down on the bed. "Where's Jasper?"

Jasper had turned off the taps a few seconds before Deena opened the door, thank goodness. "He's downstairs," I lied. Having a pistol pointed at one caused all sorts of physical reactions. My heart was fluttering, and my voice sounded as shaky as my legs felt. I licked my lips and tried again. I hoped my wavering voice had carried into the bath. "He's gone to call Inspector Longly."

"Oh, there's no need for that," Deena said. "The inspector is already here." Her cheeks were flushed, but otherwise she seemed exactly as she had when I'd seen her earlier in the hallway. Her narrow face didn't look the least bit perturbed, and she held the barrel of the gun steady on my midsection.

"What do you mean Inspector Longly's here?"

"I telephoned the police station with a tip." The

whiffle of Mr. Quigley expanding his wings sounded from under the cloth cover, and the cage rocked slightly. Deena steadied it with her free hand.

"Then you should put that gun down straightaway," I said. "The police tend to frown on people waving a pistol about. I'm sure if you put it away, everything will be fine. No harm done." My voice held a trace of Sonia's determinedly jolly tone.

Deena stood in front of the door to the hall. I was too far from the bell pull, so I couldn't summon a maid, and the bath door was on the other side of the room. I was marooned in an area of the room where the tables and chairs were out of my reach. The closest thing to me was the bed, which was a long stride away, but besides Mr. Quigley's cage, it only had fringed pillows on it.

"Inspector Longly will never see this pistol. And I'm not putting it away, so you can drop that false chipper tone. Now," she said briskly, "there's no need to pretend you don't know exactly what's happened. I came upstairs for my handkerchief and saw Jasper lingering near my room, so I hid behind the tapestry in the hall and heard you talking about my shoes. You both were so lost in your conversation that you walked right by and didn't notice me. I do hate to depart Parkview so abruptly—such bad manners, but it can't be helped. I ran back to my room, gathered up a few things." She glanced toward the birdcage. "I can't leave Mr. Quigley behind. And I made sure I had this sweet little thing." She waggled the pistol.

She flicked a glance at her wristwatch. "I don't have long. I must slip away while the inspector is busy, and

I've left him plenty to do. He'll have to collect the photograph from Peter's room and arrest him. Then he'll—"

"What photograph?" I asked, straining to listen for movement in the bath or the hallway. Had Jasper slipped out through the door that opened onto the corridor? Was he poised on the other side of the bedroom door, waiting for the right moment to burst into my room?

"The photo I kept back from the album." She smiled, but there was no warmth in her expression, only a mocking sadness, which accentuated her resemblance to a mournful saint's icon. "Poor Olive. You've worked so hard, running around, trying to figure things out, but I'm about to undo it all. The photograph of Mr. Payne came in handy. It's a nice touch, I think, putting it in Peter's room." She tilted her head to the side, and her dangling diamond earring swung away from her cheek. "It's such a shame I've had to cut things short. It would have been so satisfying to give Inspector Longly another dead body to investigate. But I just don't have time to arrange an *accident* and have you drown in the bath."

"What? You can't be serious."

"Of course I'm serious, but I've abandoned that idea. Once I heard you and Jasper speculating outside my room, I knew I had to cut my plans back. It would be too cumbersome to take care of you *and* Mr. Rimington," she said as if killing two people was such a bother. "I would have rather liked to give him a push at the top of the stairs, though."

"Like you shoved Peter," I said, the truth of what had happened during the picnic dawning on me.

"That was a miscalculation, my one mistake. Pushing Mr. Rimington down the stairs would be a completely different situation. No handy underbrush to grab onto there to break his fall. I never make the same mistake twice, that's why I'm good at this—quite good, in fact. It's my talent you know, murders. I can't sing or play, and I wasn't clever in school, but planning a murder isn't difficult. It just takes a little thought to work out all the details, and the ability to adapt when the situation changes."

For someone who was on a time schedule, she was quite chatty, but I could tell she was relishing every word. I supposed being a murderer—a successful one—put one in a lonely position. You couldn't brag or show off. No one else knew of your brilliance, which wasn't a happy thought for me. I said, "But Jasper knows you killed Mr. Payne and your cousin—yes, we figured that bit out as well. Whatever you do to me—" The words stuck in my mouth, but I went on, "Jasper knows, and he'll tell Inspector Longly."

She waved her free hand, flicking away my argument. "Inspector Longly may suspect me, but *he* won't survive the night. You don't believe me? That's foolish. I've found people are eager to help me if they're rewarded properly. A thick wad of pound notes can persuade even the most loyal staff to do me a favor. The turn down by the bridge is extremely dangerous. The inspector and whoever is in the motor with him—which will be Peter, of course—won't survive. It will close up everything perfectly. That sharp turn by the river . . ." She made a tsking sound as she shook her head. "Their motor won't be the first to crash there, will it? I heard the servants talking about it. Two other people died there within the last few years. So sad to add to the tally, but one does what one must."

"You can't think leaving a trail of dead bodies will allow you to cover everything up?" I was aghast, and it came through in my tone, but she only widened her eyes, her face taking on an innocent look.

"But it will be an accident—a tragic, horrible accident." Her expression hardened. "That's why I can't kill you and Mr. Rimington, as much as I'd like to. Four bodies in one evening would be rather over the top."

"But the evidence—"

"Will be with me. I'll take Bobby's medical records with me tonight, and then it will only be my word against yours and Mr. Rimington's. He's only a silly old fop. No one will take him seriously."

"You shouldn't underestimate Jasper." Where was he? If he didn't show up soon, I'd be sorry I'd defended him.

Deena let out a huff. "That peacock? I've no worries there. You, on the other hand, are a concern. But while I'm in some tropical country—I've heard South America is lovely, warm and exotic and very welcoming of well-to-do foreigners—I'll hire an excellent firm of solicitors to squash any rumors or innuendo that you might circulate about me. Then I'll hire some grubby individuals who will grind your reputation into dust. When they're finished with you, no one will believe a word you say. You'll be thoroughly discredited. Now, where's the note? Is it in your little hidey-hole there in the wall? My maid told me all about the nooks and crannies behind the wainscoting. Go on—open it and get the note out, along with Bobby's file."

"Note?" I asked.

"Yes, the note." Impatience laced her tone. "You've been snooping and searching. And you said you know this house well. You must have found it."

"I don't know what you're talking about."

"Come now, you don't expect me to believe that."

"Honestly, I don't know." What was Jasper doing? Had he gone to the drawing room to gather reinforcements? I really had no idea what note Deena was asking about, and I didn't think I could stave her off much longer.

Deena tilted her head and said to herself, "Perhaps it was a bluff. Although, why he'd mention it with his dying breath, I don't know."

Surely, she wasn't talking about her cousin Bobby. He'd died years ago and the chances of anyone finding a note from him were miniscule. "Mr. Payne mentioned a note?"

"Yes, frustrating man. It had all gone perfectly up to that point. I *accidentally* dropped the envelope full of cash that I'd brought, he bent to retrieve it, and I smashed him on the head with the spade I'd hidden in the foliage before he arrived. It was only as I was dragging him across the conservatory floor that he murmured something about the note. Unfortunately, he didn't live long enough for me to get any more details out of him about it." She looked at her watch and blew out a little breath. "Well, I'll just have to find it myself." She motioned with the tip of the gun, flicking it toward the cupboard. "Get me Bobby's file."

I wasn't about to turn my back to her. When I didn't move, she took a few steps to the middle of the room and planted her feet on the pale green leaf pattern at the center of the oriental rug. She clasped both hands around the pistol's handle. "Go on."

I did the only thing I could think of. I squinted and said, "I think you've lost one of your earrings."

I ducked, and in the second she jerked her hand up to check her earlobe, a wet sponge came hurtling through the bath door and splotched against Deena's face.

I stayed behind the bed as she wiped the water away and whirred toward the bath. A long-handled bath brush gyrated through the air and grazed her shoulder.

She fired. A splintered hole appeared in the door-frame. Ears buzzing from the bang of the pistol, I crawled around the end of the bed, grabbed the fringe-covered edge of the carpet Deena stood on, and yanked. She stumbled sideways and knocked against the lacquered screen. The impact folded one panel back and the screen toppled, the edge of the divider's heavy oak frame falling squarely on Deena's upper leg. A snap—the sound of a bone breaking, I realized—made my stomach turn.

Jasper came out of the bath. "Are you all right?" he asked me as he kicked the pistol, which had landed a few feet away from Deena, out of her reach. She didn't seem to care about the pistol at all. She was gripping her leg and moaning.

I stood up from my crouching position. "Yes, I believe so," I said, but I pressed a hand to the bed to steady myself. The pressure on the mattress caused the birdcage to tilt and the fabric fell back, revealing Mr. Quigley. He twisted his head around, eyeing first us, then Deena.

Jasper said, "I believe Deena's passed out. Not surprising. That's a nasty break."

"What took you so long?" The rush of anxiety and fear pulsing through me made my words shrill. "Were you scrubbing your back in there?"

"Hardly. I knew you'd want to get all the details from her. I was merely giving you time to extract the truth."

Mr. Quigley squawked and flared his wings as he said, "The truth will set you free."

"Not in Deena's case," Jasper quipped, but his face changed when I didn't return his smile. "You're still upset, I see. I promise I had my sponge primed and ready the whole time." He lifted his arms. Tiny soap bubbles lined his cuffs and sudsy water ran in rivulets down his evening kit. "Thank you for defending me, by the way. Old fop, indeed!"

I grinned. "Well, you are a bit of a peacock, but you're certainly not silly or old—well, you can be silly, but I mean that in the nicest sense of the word."

"Thank you, my dear—I think." Jasper, wringing water from his cuffs, smiled as the tension between us faded. He extended an arm. I leaned against him, not minding the dampness that soaked into the back of my dress as his arm came around me.

A tap sounded on the door. "Olive," Gwen called. "Are you in there?"

"Come in," I said. Jasper stepped back and straightened his lapels as if that would make him more presentable.

The door inched open. "Olive, dreadful news—" Gwen's startled gaze went from Deena, who was still half under the Chinese screen, then to Jasper and me. "Goodness! What happened?"

"Deena killed Mr. Pay—oh, Gwen! Where's Inspector Longly?" I asked, remembering Deena's plans for him. A fresh dose of adrenaline raced through me. I had no idea if the police motor had been tampered with, but if even part of what she'd said was true . . .

Gwen blinked and drew her gaze away from Deena. "That's what I came to tell you. He's just left—with Peter. It's awful. One of the missing photographs was in Peter's room—"

I hurried around the bed. "Deena tampered with his motor. She said he'd crash at the turn by the bridge."

She stared at me a moment, then dashed around me and out of the room. She crossed the hall to the windows. The drapes ballooned as she yanked them back. Headlights swept across the darkness. "They're pulling away from the stables now." She called, "I'll catch him," as she ran down the stairs.

I took a few steps to follow her, then stopped short and looked back into my room. Jasper had picked up the gun. "Go, go. Gwen might need your help." He settled into an armchair. "I'll wait here with Miss Lacey." Jasper crossed one leg over the other. "I doubt she'll give me any trouble, but do send the police and the doctor along when you have a moment."

"I will. Thank you, Jasper."

"No worries. I like nothing better than keeping watch over an unconscious murderess. Off you go. Gwen might need you."

Gwen had always been a placid soul, progressing through life at a steady pace, but she moved faster now than I'd ever seen her. By the time I rounded the landing above the entry hall, she was already dragging one of the heavy front doors open. The cold air slapped against me as I followed her outside. The police motor's engine, a low growl, grew louder as it rounded the house.

Gwen flew down one branch of the double curving staircase to the sweep and darted into the path of the motor. It swung around the corner from the stables, and the headlights illuminated Gwen as she ran toward the car, arms waving.

The motor veered around her and careened across the lawn, bumping along over the ground until the front headlight clipped the trunk of one of the massive oaks. The motor slowed in an arcing skid that churned up the grass, then it came to a stop.

Gwen was off and running again the second motor stopped, and she beat me to it by quite a distance. When I arrived, Peter had emerged from the passenger side and was walking around to the other side, where Longly and Gwen stood shouting at each other.

". . . in the blazes were you thinking, jumping in front of us like that?" Longly's face was pale and he was gesticulating, waving his arm at the motor. "You could have been killed."

"If you'll be quiet for a moment, I'll tell you," Gwen said, her hands fisted at her sides. "It was Deena. She killed Mr. Payne." Gwen threw out her arm toward me. "Olive figured it out, as I knew she would. I don't know the details, but Deena did something to your motor to cause an accident. You might have gone into the river if I hadn't stopped you."

"So you ran out and put yourself in the motor's path?" Longly closed the distance between them but didn't lower his voice. "Of all the idiotic, foolish things—"

"I had to stop you. I love you and couldn't let you just drive off." Gwen's exasperated voice lifted over his ranting.

Longly froze, his words cutting off as if he'd been turned to stone. He studied her face for a moment, then said, "Love—?" He cleared his throat. "You love me?"

Gwen looked mortified.

"Well, there's no taking that back," I said to Gwen as I gave her a gentle shove, which brought her a few steps closer to Longly.

Her gaze was locked on Longly, and I don't think she realized I'd touched her. She had pressed both hands to her mouth, but she nodded her head.

Longly's expression softened. He put his hand on her cheek.

Peter stepped forward. "I say, I don't think that's appropriate."

Longly didn't hear him. He was completely absorbed in Gwen.

I put a hand through Peter's elbow and pulled him back toward the house. "I think they'll finally be able to work things out now. Let me tell you what's happened . . ."

CHAPTER TWENTY-FOUR

*T*he next morning as Hannah packed my luggage, I rubbed my eyes and poured myself another cup of tea. It had been the early hours of the morning before I'd retired to bed. Deena would soon be charged with Payne's murder, and we were all free to go.

After everything calmed down and Longly was able to tear himself away from Gwen, I'd been in the middle of describing Deena's missing pair of shoes to Longly when the sergeant who'd been taking notes put down his pencil and cleared his throat. "Excuse me, sir."

Longly had looked up from his notebook as the sergeant continued, "I believe I saw a shoe in the incinerator when I searched it. It was over to the side and was only somewhat charred. I didn't remove it because we were only looking for photographs at that point."

Longly had sent him to check the incinerator, and the sergeant returned with a single woman's shoe. "I could only find the one, sir," he'd said apologetically. A charred, smoky smell had come from the bundle he held—he'd wrapped his find in an old newspaper—but the shoe itself was intact, and there was enough fabric attached to the heel to show it had once been royal blue.

At that point the doctor was tending to Deena, setting her leg. Longly had told the sergeant to take Deena to the police station as soon as they finished, using one of the estate's motors because the steering on the police motor wasn't working.

I reached for the teapot as I contemplated my luggage, which Hannah had stacked by the door before she left my room. In the last few days, Payne's murder had eclipsed my worries about finding new lodgings, but with Peter cleared of suspicion, my problem of a lack of living quarters came into sharp focus again.

A tap on my door sounded, and Gwen poked her head in. "Oh, good. You're awake." She noticed my suitcase and valise. "And ready to travel, I see."

"Yes. The problem is I'm not sure where I'm going."

Gwen sat down on the bed. "Will you return to London?"

"I'll have to. I do have a few more days in Mrs. Gutler's boardinghouse. After that, I'm not sure what I'll do. Perhaps I could leave my extra trunks and boxes here?"

"Of course. And you know you can return and stay here as well—or stay on now."

"No, I couldn't do that. I'll have to press ahead until I find some kind of lodging in London, even if it is a dingy little room or a damp flat. I like what I'm doing, helping people."

"Well, you certainly helped Peter. He was off at dawn to check on his bees. Then he has a meeting later today about distributing the honey to Nether Woodsmoor and other villages in the area. There's even a possibility of selling it to shops in London."

"That's wonderful." I put my cup down. Gwen knew Peter better than anyone else. "Do you think this incident has set him back?"

Gwen considered a moment before she answered. "It was grim there for a while, but this morning he looked quite sunny and optimistic—well, as sunny and optimistic as one can look with a bruised eye. It's a horrid yellowish-green today, but that means it's nearly healed up, thank goodness." She gave a small nod. "I think he'll be fine, especially if he can continue his outdoor pursuits and take on more responsibility from Father. If he stays busy, it helps him."

Gwen reached up to brush a strand of hair behind her ear, and I sat forward. "Gwen, is that a new ring?"

A slow smile spread across her face as she extended her hand toward me, fingers splayed and palm down. "Yes, it is."

I admired the ring as she angled her hand so the small stone caught the light. "It's gorgeous," I said. "And it's just like you to ask after me first this morning, instead of telling me your news."

With her cheeks flushing a bright pink, she adjusted the stone so that it was in the center of her finger. "Lucas gave it to me last evening."

"After you saved him."

"Oh, I wouldn't say I saved him—"

"You saved him," I said emphatically. "That turn by the river is dangerous." Gwen shifted on the bed, and I could tell she was uncomfortable with the praise. "It's true," I said.

"Well, whatever the case, it finally convinced him that I loved him."

"He didn't understand that before?"

"He had some silly idea that I wouldn't want to be the wife of a policeman. As if it matters to me whether I live in Parkview Hall or in his small flat in London— which isn't damp or poky, by the way."

"I imagine not. He's one of Scotland Yard's stars, I think. He has a bright future ahead of him."

"I certainly think so."

"Where is he now?"

"He's with Ross now, examining the police motor. Ross said the new young man he hired to help in the garden a few weeks ago has disappeared." Gwen wrinkled her nose. "I probably shouldn't have told you that. I'll have to learn to be much more discreet as an inspector's wife."

"You don't have to worry about me. You know it won't go any farther."

"You are discreet, and I'm sure the news will be all over Parkview and the village in a few hours."

"So, the man is gone?"

"Yes, Ross saw him leaving the stables at a time that he had no reason to be in there. The word in the servant's hall is that he stopped into the White Duck last evening and bought a round for everyone, saying he'd had a windfall, then he caught a ride to Upper

Benning. Deena must have paid him off to sabotage the motor."

"It seems throwing money around to get what she wanted was a habit of hers."

"Well, Lucas says all the money in the world won't help her now."

A brisk rap on the door sounded, and Sonia entered, then stopped short on the threshold. "Oh, I'm sorry. I'll return later."

Gwen stood. "No, I'll leave you two." She paused at the door. "Olive, don't make any plans for June just yet."

Gwen closed the door, and Sonia took a few steps into the room, then hesitated, her hands clasped together at her waist.

"It seems there will be a double wedding in June," I said, then wished I could bite my tongue because Sonia was so set on seeing me married.

But she surprised me and only said, "I hope Gwen and the inspector are very happy together." Sonia cleared her throat. "I said some hurtful things yesterday, and I've come to apologize."

Sonia did look like someone who'd been called to the headmistress's office. I gestured to a chair for her as I said, "You're not the only one who should apologize. I had some rather dark suspicions of you, and I'm sorry for that."

Sonia sat, back straight, hands clasped together in her lap. "Now that I've had time to think about it, I can see how you might suspect I was involved in the death. I didn't understand when I asked you to help me that you were interested in finding the truth. I could only think about protecting myself, keeping my secret. But you wanted to know what really happened. I see now that you pursue truth for the people you help in the same way I'd help a patient pursue recovery."

If I hadn't been sitting down, I would have taken a seat abruptly.

Sonia gave a little laugh and looked down at her linked fingers. "You're shocked I said that. Whether or not you believe it, I do admire you. I thought marriage would be the best thing for you, but it appears you've found something that suits you." A hint of a grin crossed her face. "At least for now. Don't completely write off the married state."

"Speaking of that," I said, "I will keep your secret."

Sonia let out a sigh and her posture loosened. "You don't have to keep that secret—at least not from your father. I told him everything last night, so now I don't care if Inspector Longly discovers I was once married to Simon Adams, who eventually became Mr. Payne. It's a massive weight off my shoulders. However, the inspector doesn't seem inclined to dig deeper into the past of *Mr. Payne.* Inspector Longly said there's ample evidence against Miss Lacey."

"How did Father take the news?" I asked.

"I was so worried he'd be angry, but he wasn't cross. He was disappointed I hadn't told him—and hurt." She paused, took a deep breath, and went on, "Your father has high standards, but he's also forgiving. Cecil told me he wished I'd trusted him enough to tell him the truth, but he'd made many mistakes of his own. Things are a bit—tense—between us now, but I think we'll get through it."

"I'm glad," I said, and I meant it.

"Thank you. I appreciate that." Her worried look returned as she added, "Cecil plans to contact the bishop and explain what happened. I don't like the idea, but your father assures me that the bishop can be trusted to keep the details confidential. Cecil says that since I truly believed I was a widow when we married that everything will be fine."

"I'm sure it will be. After all, the British government believed he was dead."

"Yes, that's true," she said in a slightly more relieved tone.

Goodness, I was reassuring Sonia—that was something I'd never thought would happen. I'd always considered her an interfering, bossy interloper, but I couldn't think of her that way anymore, not now that I knew her background.

Sonia stood up abruptly and shook out her long skirts. "I must be going." She turned back from the door, hesitated, then said, "Perhaps you'll come by Tate House for a cup of tea before you return to London?"

"I'd like that very much."

She nodded, then left the room.

I put on my hat and gloves. If someone had told me when I left London that Sonia and I would reach a tentative rapport before I returned, I wouldn't have believed them. I wasn't completely sure the situation would last, but I liked it better than the tension which had always marked our relationship. I picked up my handbag and met Miss Miller in the hallway. We descended the stairs together. "Are you on your way home today?" I asked her.

"I am. That nice inspector returned my letter to me." She patted the pocket of her dress. "I plan to return to Parkview next week for a bridge tournament Caroline is hosting. Will you be here as well?"

"I don't think so." I sincerely hoped that by next week I'd be settled in new lodgings in London.

"Then goodbye, my dear." She patted my hand. "Thank you so much for your help. Now, there was a marmalade on the breakfast table this morning that was especially tasty. I think I detected a hint of honey in it. I must get the recipe before I depart . . ." She drifted off in the direction of the breakfast room.

I asked Brimble to have my bags brought down, and I was just turning away when Mr. Davis's rotund figure emerged from Uncle Leo's study. He held some papers in one hand and his pince-nez in his other. "Good morning, Miss Belgrave," he said, then without pausing for me to answer, he turned to the butler. "Where is Sir Leo?"

"He is with Mr. Peter on the north grounds of the estate."

"Then is the inspector still here?"

"No, but I believe he will return later today."

"Notify me immediately when he arrives. I must speak to him. It's urgent. *Extremely* urgent."

"Very good, Mr. Davis." Brimble inclined his head and went to see to coordinating my bags.

"You seem distressed, Mr. Davis," I said.

He tapped the paper with his pince-nez. "This is evidence. It must have sat on my desk for several days, which is disturbing when one thinks of it."

"Evidence? What do you mean?"

"It's a letter written by Mr. Payne."

CHAPTER TWENTY-FIVE

"*M*ay I?" I asked Mr. Davis.

"Certainly." He handed it to me as he said, "Sir Leo left it on my desk for me to file. He noted on the envelope that it contained an invoice for the maps, but that"—he tapped the paper with his glasses—"is different from business correspondence. *Quite* different."

I looked up from skimming the letter to the envelope Mr. Davis was waving. It was the envelope I'd seen on his desk when I telephoned Boggs.

"I think I know what happened," I said slowly. "There was another envelope in Mr. Payne's room. I saw it when Inspector Longly had the room searched. It contained an invoice for the maps. Inspector Longly thought it was a copy of an invoice, but I bet what happened is that there was only one invoice, not an invoice and a copy of it. Mr. Payne must have used the writing paper from the desk to compose an invoice. Then he used the same writing paper to write this letter.

He put both pieces of paper in envelopes, then picked up the wrong envelope and gave it to Uncle Leo, thinking it was the invoice for the maps. Did Uncle Leo open the envelope?"

"No, he never opens invoices. He always sends them directly to me."

"So this is the note Deena was looking for."

"The young woman who—er—caused so much unpleasantness?"

"Yes, she searched Mr. Payne's room the night after he was killed, looking for this letter." I read through the note again more slowly.

I, Vincent Payne, witnessed Deena Lacey suffocate her cousin, Bobby Stanton, in November 1914. This event occurred when I was a patient recovering from war injuries at Parkview Hall. I was assigned to the mahogany room, which I shared with Mr. Stanton.

I was rather done in and under medication quite a lot, but I was aware of nurses and doctors arriving and departing as well as occasional visitors such as Miss Lacey. She came to read to us and write our letters. One day I was drifting in and out of consciousness when I thought I saw her leaning over Mr. Stanton, holding a pillow to his face.

My memories of that time were once hazy, but my visit to Parkview has brought that time into focus. Perhaps I had suppressed the memory because there were so many other horrible things I was trying not to remember as well, but when I stood there in the mahogany room and Miss Lacey was there as well, it all came back to me like a film at the cinema.

I'd been given a dose of medicine that morning and felt lethargic. I opened my eyes—barely slit them—and saw Miss Deena Lacey standing beside Mr. Stanton's bed. I tried to stay awake, but my eyes kept closing. I remember thinking it was a shame I wouldn't be able to talk to the young lady. I must have drifted off, but I heard a noise—a strange noise—a body shifting, thrashing about. I opened my eyes again, and she was pressing a pillow onto Stanton's face. Then she stepped back and watched him for a moment. I was going to call out, but when I saw her watching him—checking to make sure he was gone—I lost my nerve. I closed my eyes again, so she'd think I was asleep. I was afraid I might be next if she knew I'd seen her. When I opened my eyes again, she was gone. A nurse came in, gave me another injection, and hushed me when I tried to tell her what had happened. The medicine took effect, and I couldn't stay awake.

The next time I awoke, the nurse told me Mr. Stanton had been moved to another room, and Miss Lacey hadn't been in to visit for days. I kept quiet because I thought I was cracking up. I didn't want to be one of those lads who couldn't handle themselves. I thought the whole thing must have been a horrible nightmare.

It was a month later when I learned Mr. Stanton had indeed died. By then, I was questioning my own memories. Had I actually seen what I thought I'd seen? Was it the medicine? Had it caused me to imagine things? And what happened to Miss Lacey? I didn't see her again at Parkview Hall.

I realize now it was no hallucination. When I told her

about my memory, her reaction told me everything I needed to know in one startled glance. It was true. She had *killed Bobby Stanton, and I'd seen her do it. I'm writing this down as a sort of insurance policy. Miss Lacey is going to give me a tidy little payment to ensure my silence—and I'll tell her about this letter—but if anything happens to me, it'll be Deena who did it.*

I looked up from the letter. "How horrifying."

Mr. Davis put a hand to his necktie. "Indeed."

A throat cleared behind us, and Inspector Longly stepped forward. "Miss Belgrave. I see you are, as usual, in the midst of the most exciting revelations."

"But I missed one important bit of news. Congratulations on your engagement."

He blushed just as Gwen had done and smiled widely. He looked truly happy as he said, "Thank you."

"I look forward to having you as a cousin-in-law."

He looked stunned as if he hadn't thought about that. I handed him the note. "You'll find this fascinating reading," I said and described how the note and the invoice must have been switched.

Brimble approached me as I finished and asked, "Shall I have your bags loaded into your motor, Miss Belgrave?"

"Yes, please do."

As I left, Longly was escorting Mr. Davis back to the study and asking questions about the envelope and letter.

A few minutes later, I'd said my goodbyes to Aunt

Caroline and Gwen. When I inquired after Jasper, Brimble told me Jasper had already breakfasted and gone out for a short stroll.

"How unusual," I said. Jasper wasn't typically so enthusiastic about exercise. "Well, I'm sure I'll see him in London." I'd send a note around to him once I was back in town. Perhaps we'd have tea at the Savoy.

The Morris was brought around, and I was halfway down the staircase on my way to the sweep in front of the house when Gigi called my name. She gave Captain Inglebrook's arm a squeeze and motioned for him to stay outside the door, then ran down to me. "Olive, you can't leave. Remember there was something I want to speak to you about?"

"I'm sorry. I completely forgot with everything else that happened."

"I made an exception to my rule about rising before noon specifically for you. I knew you'd be off as soon as possible, and I must talk to you. My situation is merely a trifle, but I'd like your help."

"My help?"

"It's Grandmother Pearl. She thinks someone is trying to kill her," she said in the same tone someone would use to describe a child who believed unicorns existed.

"You think she's imagining things."

Gigi tilted her head back and forth as if she couldn't make up her mind. "Well, she's difficult enough that someone probably does want to kill her. The thought has crossed my mind, believe me, but I've never acted on it." Gigi smiled at her own joke, but after the situa-

263

tion at Parkview, suspecting relatives of murder struck a little too close to home. Gigi didn't notice my subdued reaction, and went on, "But yes, her imagination has . . . gotten away from her lately. I understand you're in a bit of a bind as far as living quarters?"

"That's true."

"Then why don't you come and stay at my flat in London? I have plenty of room. We can visit Grandmother, and you can help her understand she's simply mistaken."

"Sounds intriguing, and I love intriguing situations."

"Excellent. I convinced Captain Inglebrook he should spend some time in London as well. We can attend parties and shop and dine at the best restaurants."

"I'll come stay with you for a few days. Say, starting next week?"

"Perfect." She leaned in and kissed the air near my cheek. "Goodbye, darling. See you soon." She ran back upstairs in a flurry of swishing fabric.

I descended the stairs and climbed into the Morris. I was about to put the motor in gear when Jasper appeared on the passenger side and propped an arm on the door. "Got room for one more?"

"Of course. Would you like me to run you up to London?"

"Oh, it's not for me." He stepped back and lifted Mr. Quigley's cage. "Aunt Caroline thinks you and Mr. Quigley have quite an affinity. She'd like you to take him to London. She says she'll send his larger cage as soon as you give her your new location."

"She wants me to take Mr. Quigley?" I barely had a place for myself to lay my own head. I couldn't take charge of a parrot as well. "But he'd be so much happier in the conservatory."

"I floated that idea, but Aunt Caroline said only for short visits. She isn't taking on a parrot as a pet."

"Well, I'm not either." Mr. Quigley cocked his head to the side and let out a clicking sound. I sighed. "I suppose I can keep him until I find a new home for him."

"Brilliant. And since you're on your way to London, I will catch a ride with you as far as Upper Benning. My motor should be repaired by now. That is, if you have the space," he said, his gaze ranging over the luggage stacked in the seat.

"There's always room for you, Jasper."

"That is good news," he said softly.

I smiled at him, catching the extra layer of meaning his tone gave the words. I handed him my valise so he could shift it around to make room. "I don't have room for a parrot *and* Grigsby, though."

Jasper waved a hand. "Grigsby is returning to London on the train. He doesn't like riding with me for some reason."

Once his bags were stowed and Mr. Quigley's cage was positioned between us on the front seat, I took off down the drive. "So, Jasper," I said, "have you ever considered owning a parrot?"

Want to know when the next High Society Lady Detective book is coming out? Sign up for Sara's Notes and News Updates at SaraRosett.com/signup and get her mystery book recommendations and news about sales and discounts.

THE STORY BEHIND THE STORY

$\mathcal{T}$hank you for joining Olive for another mystery among the high society set. One of my favorite things about writing Olive's adventures is the research. Because the mystery for this book had its roots in the past, I delved into World War I history and read about life in the trenches as well as on the home front. *Lady Almina and the Real Downtown Abbey: The Lost Legacy of Highclere Castle* by the Countess of Carnarvon provided the inspiration for the descriptions of Parkview Hall's transformation into a hospital for injured servicemen.

Shortly after war was declared in 1914, Lady Almina converted Highclere Castle into a place of healing and recovery to fill an urgent need for a country unprepared to care for the enormous number of the wounded. I was surprised to learn that a broken femur, like Mr. Payne's injury, was often a death sentence. It was the use of a specially designed splint, called the Thomas splint, that dramatically increased the survival rate.

Mr. Payne's unique fraud of selling antique maps with forged signatures is based on the Lincoln Forgeries, a scam that Eugene Field II carried out in real life. He inherited books from his grandfather and forged Abraham Lincoln's signature on them. Eventually, he took on a partner and branched out, forging Lincoln's signature as well as Rudyard Kipling's, Theodore Roosevelt's, and Samuel Clemens's on maps, books, and other documents during the 1920s and 1930s. It's truly ironic that these forgeries are now sought after by collectors. It seemed just the sort of fraud that Mr. Payne would get up to. Forging paintings would be far too much work for him! Adding signatures to old maps and visiting country houses to pass them off to unsuspecting collectors—that was something that would appeal to a lazy conman.

I also did a deep dive into conservatories in British country homes. I modeled Parkview Hall on Chatsworth House. Chatsworth's orangery is now the estate's shop, and it was fun to browse among the books and tea towels when I visited there and imagine what it must have been like when orange trees filled the room. Chatsworth was also home to one of the most dramatic "glass houses" in the world. Constructed under gardener and architect Sir Joseph Paxton, Chatsworth's Great Conservatory was over 200 feet long and over 100 feet wide. It was the largest glass structure in the world when it was built in 1836. Heated with boilers that fueled 12,000 lamps, it was a forerunner of the Crystal Palace, which Paxton would go on to design. Sadly, the Great Conservatory had to be destroyed during the Great War because the cost of maintaining it was too high. The conservatory at Parkview isn't as grand as the Great Conservatory, but I did have the amazing conservatories with their lush tropical plants in mind when writing about the conservatory in this book.

A few other interesting tidbits of research popped up, including the Chanel suit that Deena wears on the picnic. Coco Chanel is famous for designing comfortable and stylish clothing with jersey, a knit material that had previously been used for men's undergarments. Her famous tweed suit appeared in the early 1920s. I found an image of a tweed Chanel suit published in 1924, which popularized the new casual style. I knew Deena, who was on the cutting edge of fashion, would have snapped it up at its debut in Paris.

Another research rabbit hole I went down was about soldiers' reading habits during the war. Books were supplied to the troops, and the commanding officers reported their men had a preference for Jane Austen, which doesn't surprise me at all. What better way to escape the chaos of war than with one of Austen's novels, which are full of gentle humor and deep human emotion. Another reading favorite during the 1920s was *The Thirty-Nine Steps*, which was published in 1915. I'd only seen the black-and-white Hitchcock film version of the novel, but after learning it was such a popular book, I read it while researching *Murder in Black Tie*. One caveat about the book: a character in *The Thirty-Nine Steps* has jarringly anti-Semitic attitudes, which are eventually discredited. The breathless pace of one of the first "man on the run" stories was so popular, it influenced movies like *North by Northwest* and *The Bourne Identity*.

Thanks again for reading *Murder in Black Tie!* Check out my Pinterest board for Murder in Black Tie to see more details about the places and people that inspired the book. Sign up for my Notes and News Updates at SaraRosett.com/signup to get my reading recommendations as well as updates about upcoming books and sale news. I'd love to stay in touch!

ABOUT THE AUTHOR

USA Today bestselling author Sara Rosett writes light-hearted mysteries for readers who enjoy atmospheric settings, fun characters, and puzzling whodunits.

She is the author of the High Society Lady Detective historical mystery series as well as three contemporary cozy series, the Murder on Location series, the On the Run series, and the Ellie Avery series. Sara also teaches an online course, How to Outline A Cozy Mystery.

Publishers Weekly called Sara's books, "satisfying," "well-executed," and "sparkling." Sara loves to get new stamps in her passport and considers dark chocolate a daily requirement. Find out more at SaraRosett.com.

Connect with Sara
www.SaraRosett.com

Made in the
USA
Monee, IL